I0718222

# DEFENDING THE BACKFIELD

---

## LA WOLVES DEFENSE
### BOOK 1

## CADENCE KEYS

Copyright © 2023 by Cadence Keys

All rights reserved.

No part of this book may be reproduced in any form or by any electronic or mechanical means, including information storage and retrieval systems, without written permission from the author, except for the use of brief quotations in a book review.

This book is a work of fiction. Names, characters, places, and incidents are a product of the author's imagination. Locales and public names are sometimes used for atmospheric purposes. Any resemblances to actual people, living or dead, businesses, companies, events, institutions, or locales are entirely coincidental. Any trademarks, service marks, product names, or named features are assumed to be the property of their respective owners and are used only for reference.

Editors: Happily Editing Anns

Sensitivity Reader: Rikki Perez

Cover Design: Kate Farlow, Y'all. That Graphic

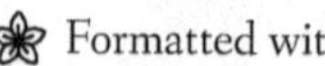 Formatted with Vellum

*For the survivors and those who never gave up hope. You are absolutely deserving of your own happily every after.*

# PLAYLIST

"Last Hope"—Paramore
"Train Wreck"—James Arthur
"Save Yourself"—Birdy
"Alive"—Sia
"Salvation"—Gabrielle Aplin
"Don't You Worry"—Oh Wonder
"Like That"—JP Saxe
"Thick Skin"—Leona Lewis
"Naked"—Brielle Von Hugel
"Break Me"—Jewel
"Always Been You"—Shawn Mendes
"Stop Runnin'"—LOKRE
"Carry You"—Ruelle, Fleurie
"Hang On A Little Longer"—UNSECRET, Ruelle
"Little Did I Know"—Julia Michaels

Listen now on Spotify

# FOREWORD

This book contains references of domestic abuse (not between the main characters). Please take care of your mental health first and foremost.

If you or someone you love is experiencing domestic abuse, please know there is help. Please call the National Domestic Violence Hotline at 800-799-7233.

# PREFACE

"It's always darkest before the dawn."
–Thomas Fuller

ONE

# Danae

My eyes shift to the rearview mirror, my heart racing as I take a right turn and then another. The headlights that have been behind me for several miles continue straight, and a relieved breath expels from my lungs.

He hasn't found me.

I continue taking random turns, just in case, before I finally pull up to the garage of the house I'm renting.

I found the listing on Craigslist, which probably wasn't the safest choice, but anything beats Mitch finding me, and I was sick of always staying in cheap, disgusting motels. The rental belongs to an older couple who travel around the country and use the money to maintain the house should they ever decide to move back into it. They didn't ask me prying questions and let me pay with cash, so it was a perfect arrangement. But I've learned to never get too comfortable anywhere I stay because it's never for long. If the past year is any indication, it could be anywhere from a week to four months. It just depends on how long it takes him to find me.

And he always finds me.

My breathing accelerates as my heart starts to race again, the edges of my vision going blurry as panic washes over me. I can still feel the phantom ache in my ribs and remember how my face was so swollen I was hardly recognizable.

All because I smiled at the store clerk who packed our groceries for us in the checkout line.

The only reason I'm even alive is because our elderly neighbor, Mrs. Crawford, stopped by with a pie after Mitch had left to go hang out with his friends. She peeked in the window when I didn't answer the door and saw the blood on the floor in the kitchen. She used the spare key I'd given her in case of emergencies to get in the house and call 911.

Something she paid for dearly.

There's no proof of course, but when she died a week later, I knew it wasn't by natural causes like the coroner suggested.

Due to the severity of my injuries, an officer came down to see if I wanted to press charges. But I couldn't. All pressing charges would do is put me in the spotlight for his rage.

Believe me; I'd already tried.

He beat me so severely afterward, I was forced to take a week's vacation from my job because there was no way I could hide the damage he'd inflicted.

Of course, the damage on the outside is nothing compared to how he beat me down mentally.

It wasn't until Mrs. Crawford died that I realized how far he could go.

So, I did the only thing I could think of.

I wrote him a note that it was over, and then I ran.

When I first met Mitchell Westcott III, I thought I'd won the boyfriend lottery. I didn't know what I'd done to deserve a man who was so charming and generous. He spoiled me and lulled me into his world bit by bit, until the only thing I saw was him.

He was so smooth in his manipulations that I didn't even notice how isolated I'd become from my friends until it was too late. My family was mostly nonexistent. My mom had died in a car accident when I was eighteen, and I'd never known my dad. I met my grandparents once when I was about five, but they were cold people and my mom had decided it was better for us both if we stayed away from them.

I sometimes wonder if things with Mitch would've turned out different if I'd had more family ties. If I had more people who cared about me, would he have taken the time to pursue me the way he did until he controlled every aspect of my life?

I guess it's silly to live in a world of what if.

He kept me in the dark about his true character until I had no one but him. Sometimes, I look back on our early days together, and the self-loathing nearly swallows me whole. How did I not see it coming? How did I not notice him controlling my life? Yes, it was in small ways, but still.

I should've noticed. I should've seen the red flags. They were all there. Looking back now, I can see them clearly. But I guess what they say is true; hindsight is 20/20.

I glance behind me, checking the neighborhood for any signs of being followed before I enter the house and lock the deadbolt. I quickly make sure all the blinds are closed. I miss having daylight stream across my skin while I'm inside, but I can't risk him seeing me if he were to drive by. Who knows how long I have before he finds me this time, but I'm not about to make it any easier for him.

I start putting away the groceries I just picked up and

then get started on dinner, my gaze periodically scanning the room, my body half-braced for the possibility of seeing Mitch standing there.

I thought by now it would get easier, but after eighteen months on the run from him, I've learned that the panic thrumming just underneath the surface of my skin will probably never completely go away.

Maybe it's safer to always have the adrenaline of fear sizzling in me. It keeps my senses sharp and focused on staying one step ahead of him.

I'm halfway through eating dinner when my phone rings. My grip tightens on my fork and the blood in my veins freezes as the ringing continues. Goose bumps break out across my skin as my fear spikes.

Only one person has that phone number, and she was instructed only to use it in case of a life-and-death emergency.

I drop my fork and jump up from my chair to the phone charging on the side table. The unfamiliar sound sends both fear and excitement shooting through my body. It's an odd sensation that I don't have time to process. I press accept and bring the phone to my ear. I don't speak, waiting to hear my cousin's voice. Mitch never knew about her, and she and I had rarely talked, so I'd thought she'd be safe.

But all I hear is silence, and that feeling of dread increases until it's nearly suffocating.

I tip the phone so whoever's on the other end can't hear how my breath is coming out in terrified pants. If Mitch got to my cousin, then he's escalating, and he's found the only person I had left.

I'm right on the verge of saying Amy's name when I hear a heavy exhale and the clicking of a tongue.

"You should've stopped running in Houston, baby girl."

His voice sends ice straight to my heart, freezing my body.

"Where's Amy?" My voice cracks, giving away that he still commands this fear which never leaves me alone. But I can't focus on that until I know my cousin's safe.

She's stayed off his radar all this time. Why now?

His silence worries me.

"Mitch, where's Amy?"

He chuckles. "God, baby girl, I've missed hearing you say my name. I can't wait to hear you scream it again as I watch the light in your eyes fade away."

I grit my teeth—this isn't his first death threat. "Where the fuck is Amy?"

"Don't worry, baby girl. You'll be joining her soon. I hear Boston is nice this time of year."

Whatever strength I had left evaporates in an instant. He knows where I am.

I quickly hang up the phone, fingers shaking and tears streaming down my cheeks. My body collapses against the wall as his words land heavy on top of me.

He's killed Amy. I'm sure of it. His threat made that perfectly clear.

With unsteady limbs, I push myself up and race through the house, picking up the few items I left out and grabbing my always-packed bag. I send an email to the owner of the house explaining that my situation has changed and I'm terminating our agreement. With one last glance at the house I'd hoped would be home for a little longer, I summon as much strength as I can muster and walk to the nearest gas station, leaving my now-useless cell phone on the counter—there's no need for it anymore. I have no one else to rely on but myself. It's a two-mile walk, and I'm freezing by the time I make it inside and ask the gas station attendant if I can use his phone.

I call a random cab company and ask for them to take me to the airport. At the ticket counter, I ask the agent for the next domestic flight out of Boston.

She scans her computer. "It looks like we have a flight to New York, but"—she squints at the screen and then checks the delicate watch on her wrist—"I don't think you'd make that one by the time you got through security." She types on her computer, and I have to actively fight against my body's desire to fidget and look around at the people behind me to make sure familiar ice-blue eyes aren't watching my every move.

Her eyes light up. "I've got a flight to LA that leaves in an hour. Does that work?"

"I'll take it."

# TWO

# Gabe

The opposing tight end glances at our defense on the line of scrimmage, before his gaze moves past them and he stares me down from his crouched position. I smirk, taunting him with my eyes and causing him to narrow his gaze like he's cursing me in his head—which he probably is. My job as a strong safety is to defend the backfield, and I'm fucking good at it. This guy won't get past me.

The ball snaps, and bodies move like a gun just went off to start a race. I keep my eyes on my target, but I also know how important it is to be aware of my surroundings. When you've been playing football as long as I have, it becomes a sixth sense. The tight end I'm watching looks up in the air, and I push forward faster while keeping my head tilted up to see the trajectory of the ball. It sails through the air, heading directly for my target.

Not today. Today that ball is mine.

With another push, I surge forward and leap into the air, my arm extended as far as it'll go. My fingertips touch the pigskin, and it's pure instinct that causes me to flick my wrist enough to tip it toward me instead of its intended target. As my body begins to descend back to the ground, my hand finds purchase on the ball and I tuck it to my chest, effectively ending their play.

The Wolves are in possession now.

The ref calls it, and my boys surge around me, all of us high on the game, adrenaline pulsing through our veins. Victory is so close we can taste it.

We're having our best season yet, and it's all because we've found our stride as a team. Our offense has been strong for a few years, but our defense was missing something. Then, two years ago, Tyler Russell was traded to the Wolves as a free safety and he teamed up with me, Romel Watson, and Dominic Smith—both strong cornerbacks—in a way that turned our defense into the talk of the league. We got dubbed the Fierce Four, and every season since, we've gotten more unstoppable.

This is our year to go all the way; I can feel it.

The game continues on, Romel, Dom, and Ty always in sync with me. We stop the opposing team's forward progress so many times their quarterback has a fit right on the field—prima donna. We win the game by a landslide and exit the field on cloud nine. Any win causes a surge of adrenaline, but there's nothing like a win on your home turf.

The locker room is mayhem as we all hoot and holler. Dom—the team party boy—starts a chant that has all the players laughing and shouting at the top of their lungs. Jack Fuller, our QB and captain, joins him, helping rev up the energy until it's damn near deafening.

Fuck, I love my life.

"Alright, alright, settle down now," Coach Denton yells, his voice stern, but with a smile on his face. He's followed in by the other coaching staff, including the defensive line coach—and first female coach for the LA Wolves—Alison

Fairbright. She doesn't get enough credit for her role in the creation of the Fierce Four. I'm not even sure she realizes that we wouldn't be what we are without her guidance. It's why we defend her more than any of the other players. She turned us into legends, whether she realizes it or not.

A hush falls over the room as Coach Denton stands before us. "You did good out there, but don't let it go to your head. You've got a lot of games left until playoffs. It's too early to celebrate just yet."

His gaze sweeps across the room, making sure we all understand what he's saying, then he nods, turns, and goes into his office. The second the door closes we all go crazy again.

We know better than to get too cocky, but that doesn't mean we can't celebrate one hell of a win.

Dom saunters over to me and slaps me hard on the back. "Come on, we're going out for drinks."

I arch a brow and lean on my knee. "Who's 'we'?"

I know damn well Romel is going straight home to his barely two-year-old daughter. He's hardly gone out since his wife, Sydney, died from cancer shortly after their daughter, Kaylee, was born. They'd been high school and college sweethearts, and I'd never met two people more compatible. Syd found out in her third trimester that she had cancer, and adamantly refused to do any treatments that would threaten her baby. By the time Kaylee was born, it had spread through most of her body and was terminal. She only lasted weeks before it took her.

If I could've saved Romel the pain of losing the love of his life, I would've. It killed Dom, Ty, and me to see him so broken. But there was one guiding light that kept him from being completely consumed by his grief—his daughter. It's no secret she's his priority and the reason he gets up in the morning. In fact, there are days I wonder how long it'll be before he retires to make her his sole focus.

Dom gestures to Ty and a couple of the other single guys. Most of the guys who are in relationships tend to go straight home to their wives or girlfriends after a game. These days, it seems like more and more guys are joining the coupled-up crowd; I swear we're dropping like flies.

Not that I'd be opposed to having the kind of love guys like Jack Fuller seem to have. Lord knows I'm jealous as hell of Luke Carter and his girl, Emma. I got the chance to dance with her at Jack and Paige's wedding, and if I'd thought I had even a sliver of a chance, I would've tried to steal her away from Luke. But there was no denying who her heart belongs to; it was written all over her face.

"Come on, man. How long's it been since you got some pussy?" Dom asks.

I cringe on the inside. I have sisters, and if they heard me talk like that, they'd slap me upside the head. Don't even get me started on my mom's reaction.

There are some things that get said in a locker room that no family member should be privy too.

He shakes my shoulder as if he can shake me into going. I don't particularly want to go out—I'm kind of over the party scene that he loves—but I don't really want to go home to an empty house either.

"Alright, I'll go."

Dom raises his hands like he just scored a touchdown. "That's right. Let's gooooo!" he hollers, getting a couple of other rowdy guys to join him in chanting. I shake my head at him and then make my way to the showers.

By the time we're all cleaned up and get to the club, it's already nearing midnight, but adrenaline from a win doesn't fade for hours, so we're all still hyped up. We skip the line and head straight to the door where the bouncer shakes our hands and slaps us on the back.

"Huge fan. You guys killed it tonight!" he says with a smile before letting us in. We all thank him, and then any chance of hearing him is drowned out by the heavy bass of the music. Lights flash across a black floor where people dance.

Dom wraps one arm around me and the other around Ty. "First round's on me, boys. Tonight, we party!" He heads to the bar while Ty and I hang back, watching the scene unfold. Clubs aren't really my thing, but I'll go out every once in a while. Dom parties hard—maybe harder than he should—and always knows the best places to go, so the rare times I do go out like this, it's always with him.

"Where do you think Alayna is tonight?" Ty calls out, his gaze still staring out at the dance floor.

Alayna is Dom's best friend. Ty's convinced there has to be something there, but I've never heard Dom talk about her romantically and he fucks pretty much any woman in a skirt, which I can't see Alayna putting up with if there was any chance of them as a couple.

"Not sure. Why? You trying to get in her pants?" I ask.

Ty's laugh is loud enough to be heard clearly over the music. "Hah, fat chance. Dom would fucking kill me."

Before I can say anymore, Dom comes back over and gestures with his head toward a set of stairs, a mischievous grin on his face. "Come on, gentlemen. I've got a little somethin' special for ya."

We follow him like we would on the field and head up the stairs. There are doors along the right side, and he stops at one about halfway down. With a dramatic flourish that has me shaking my head at his antics, he swings the door open and shouts, "Daddy's here, ladies. Who wants to sit on my lap?"

He enters the room like a king, arms stretched wide, and a few women flock to him while the others are already busy sitting on the laps of other teammates that managed to get here before we did. A waitress comes in with champagne, and both Ty and I take a glass. Another woman comes up to Ty and runs a finger from the collar of his shirt down to his belly button while her bottom lip is trapped between her teeth. Her eyes promise a night of debauchery if he wants it, and a quick glance at one of my closest friends tells me he's not at all opposed. She tugs on his shirt, and his mouth falls to hers in a salacious kiss that makes me avert my gaze. She lets out a moan, and by the time I glance up at them, she's already pulling him toward a darker corner.

He turns to me with a pleased grin on his face. "Life can't get any better than this."

I watch him walk away and then step back when another waitress enters the room. Ty's words reverberate around my head, and as much as I know I *should* be enjoying this, I'm just...not. Nights like this were hot when we were rookies, but now I want a woman who is all mine. I want a woman who looks at me the way Emma looks at Luke. I want a woman to come home to after a game. One I can ravage on every surface of my house until her legs are jelly and she needs me to carry her around.

I don't think I'm going to find that woman here. And the idea of hooking up with a stranger is less than appealing tonight.

I pull out my phone and shoot a text to Dom and Ty—not interested in interrupting them right now—and then head home.

I don't know where the woman I'm meant to be with is, but I trust my gut that I'll know when I find her.

# THREE

# Danae

His finger traces her lip, his eyes heated with so much love, her heart flutters in her chest.

"You were made for me," he whispers before his lips take hers in a kiss that causes her toes to curl in her beat-up sneakers.

Tears well in her eyes as she breaks the kiss and pushes him away. "Don't. Y-you can't say that. It's not true."

His brow furrows and where a soft smile graced his handsome face, worry now resides. "It is true," he declares adamantly. "I love you, Clara."

The tears fall now and her heart breaks because she's waited her whole life for those three words. For someone— anyone—to love her, and now she's found it with the one man she can't have. Being with her would ruin his family name, his reputation, his business. It would ruin his life.

She'd never wish that on the man who holds her entire heart—even if he'll never know it.

"I want to break up. This was just supposed to be a quick fling, but you've clearly developed more feelings than I have, and I think we should end it."

*It's the worst lie she's ever told, and the heartbreak on his face hurts more than if someone had taken a dull kitchen knife and shoved it straight through her heart, forcing her to bleed out slowly.*

"Break's over!"

I startle and my heart races as my eyes snap up to see my boss, Tony, staring me down. I glance at my watch and then back at him. "I still have five minutes."

"Not anymore. We're packed. You need to get out here."

I stick a receipt in my book—an old favorite that is nearly falling apart but never fails to rip my heart out and piece it back together with a hope I have no right to have— and stand up, stretching out my sore muscles. This is my third double shift this week, and I'm fucking exhausted, but I need the money.

Speaking of...

"Hey Tony, you said you'd pay me tonight," I remind him, putting a little weight into my tone. "I need that money so I can pay my rent."

His jaw clenches and his hard eyes stare at me. I swallow down my nerves and force myself to remain staring at him even as my fight-or-flight response starts to tingle underneath my skin. He looks too much like Mitch when he gets that hard look in his eyes.

He gestures for me to follow him, so I do. He guides us to the back office and shuffles around some papers before handing me an envelope with cash. It feels lighter than it should—thinner too. I look inside and count the bills before trying to calm my heart that is now racing for a completely different reason.

"This isn't even half of what you owe me."

"That's all you're getting."

"You said you'd pay me minimum wage," I implore, hating the edge of panic filtering into my voice.

He shrugs with an air of nonchalance that makes me wish I was a violent person so I could kick him in his nuts and make him feel the slightest amount of terror I feel right now. This won't cover food let alone the rent for the cheapest motel I could find where they'd let me pay cash without giving a name.

This is the downside of working under the table. The tips at this job are okay, but not enough to live off. This pittance certainly won't cut it.

"Tony, I need my money."

"That's your money. Now get your ass back out there and take those drink orders. Open mic night is starting, and your break is officially over."

The break he stole five minutes from. I seethe as he passes by me, and helplessness crawls up my throat until it stings my nose and burns my eyes. I refuse to let the tears fall. This isn't the first time I've had a man knock me down, and I have no doubt it won't be the last, but God, I'm so fucking tired of it.

I just need to catch one break.

That's it. Just one.

I attempt to take a deep inhale, but it's hard with the weight on my chest and worry that permeates every bone. My whole body drags as I move like I'm slogging through thick mud. Open mic night is usually a busy night, but tonight it's packed, and everyone seems to be staring excitedly at the group in the upper corner near the stage. A bunch of hulking guys with beautiful women wrapped in their arms surround a gorgeous redhead as she smiles nervously and then makes her way up to the stage.

I grab my serving tray and start making my rounds,

writing down orders quickly, my feet already aching from working so long today. I'm heading back toward one of my tables with a full tray when the singer's voice fills the room like a beautiful mix between Adele and Birdy.

"Who is that?" I ask someone at the nearest table, slowing down until I'm standing completely immobilized, my gaze locked on the singer.

"She said her name was Emma Delaney. She's incredible," the girl gushes.

I'd missed her name because I'd been lost in my own thoughts, but everything's been wiped away as her words ease some of the despair that's drowning me. The emotion behind her words tells me she's not just singing something she thought about. She's singing something she's experienced.

She's been hurt, and this is her standing tall and proving it didn't kill her.

What I'd give to have the kind of strength she's displaying right now, instead of feeling like I'm one weak gust of wind away from giving up.

I'm completely lost to her song, any thought of my job or the drink orders on my tray completely forgotten. She finishes her song with a note that strikes my heart with so much emotion, I can feel a tear escape my eye. After a moment's pause, the audience goes wild, clapping and cheering for her, but no one louder than the group in the corner.

Especially the man looking at her like she's his entire world.

I know it's bad to compare your life to others'—dangerous even since you're comparing to only the snapshots you see and not the whole picture—but I've never been so jealous of someone's happiness as I am of Emma's. I watch her run down the stairs straight into his arms, their lips meeting in a deep and tender kiss. It hits me a second too late that I shouldn't be watching them like this. I have a job I need to do. My gaze moves away from them and crashes right into another, a man in their party who's not looking at Emma like everyone else, but watching me, his dark gaze curious and something else I can't quite name.

I swallow thickly, knowing I should break this weird stare-off we're having, but unable to because something about him feels safe. Like he's my own personal lighthouse while I'm stuck at sea trying to escape the raging storm. Like if I could just reach him, I'd be okay.

Which is completely ridiculous.

I know better than anyone not to trust a man, not after what Mitch put me through—what he's *still* putting me through.

With colossal effort, I look away and turn right into a customer, spilling the drinks on my tray all down his front.

"Are you fucking kidding me? Stupid bitch. Watch where you're going!"

My eyes go wide with mortification as profuse apologies prepare to pour out of my mouth. But before a single word can escape, a deep male voice comes from behind me, washing over me like a balm. "Everything okay over here?"

The guy doesn't look up from brushing the clinging stray ice off his shirt. "What the fuck does it look like?" he says and then looks up, but his glare evaporates the second he sees who was talking, and I turn my head to see the guy I was just staring at before running into this asshole.

"Holy shit," asshole guy says with awe. "You're Gabe Romero."

I glance between the two men, wondering if Gabe Romero is a name I should be familiar with. Asshole seems to think so, which doesn't bode well for me if I've now caused a scene in front of someone famous.

Gabe glances down at me like he's expecting some kind of reaction from me, and his eyes seem to light up when I just continue staring at him, hoping he'll explain so I can stop feeling like I'm missing something important.

But he doesn't get a chance because my boss storms over, staring daggers at me before he turns to the customer. "Hi, I'm the manager here. What can I do to fix this horrible accident?"

Asshole guy remembers he's supposed to be pissed and not fangirling over Gabe, and points his finger at me. "Get some competent staff. This waitress ran right into me, spilling cold drinks all over my clothes."

"I'm so sorry about that, sir," Tony says, shooting another scathing look at me. I hate that my immediate reaction is to wither under his glare. It's a trait born from years of abuse with Mitch, and one I've yet to break. "Head on over to the bar and we'll get you a drink on the house and give you a bar T-shirt to change into. Just let Stephen know Tony sent you. He'll take care of you."

The guy harrumphs and then walks over to the bar. As soon as he's out of earshot, Tony turns to me and without any fanfare or emotion whatsoever says, "You're fired."

Then, as if I now cease to exist, he turns to Gabe. "Mr. Romero. It's such an honor to have you at our establishment. Please, let us treat you to a complimentary round of drinks to make up for your trouble."

His words fade as a buzzing starts in my head, and I stare at the ground as it once again shifts out from underneath me. I haven't been in LA long and certainly haven't saved enough to afford to go somewhere else so soon. This was the first job I was able to find that would both pay me under the table and didn't require me to sell my body, and it took me three weeks to find. I've already gone through everything I saved when I was back in Boston.

Without this job, I'm royally fucked.

Even if it is one of the shittiest jobs I've ever had.

Something akin to panic starts to press on my chest to the point of pain. Is this what rock bottom feels like? I thought I'd already hit it when I was a broken pile on the floor, but this feels dangerously lower than that.

I can't breathe.

What am I going to do now?

FOUR

# Gabe

When Luke asked me a few days ago to come support Emma for her first performance in almost a year, it was a no-brainer. Emma's a sweetheart, so of course I'd support her. Besides, I haven't gone out much since the club night with Dom and needed to get out of my house. I expected to have a low-key night with some friends, drinking beer and listening to good music. I did not expect to be knocked on my ass by a mesmerizing waitress with silky, long dark hair tied back in a ponytail, curvy hips that make my fingers itch to grab them, and an ass that would make any man weep with thanks. I don't know who this woman is, but I'm desperate to find out.

Unfortunately, she looks dangerously close to passing out, her beautiful tan skin fading to a sickly white in the span of a blink. Her boss—Tony—tries to kiss my ass, but his words go completely ignored as I watch her crumple in front of me. Not physically. No, she stands frozen like a statue at the Los Angeles County Museum of Art. But I can sense this is a blow she can't withstand.

I've been watching her since we arrived over an hour

ago. There is something about her that seems fragile, but strong. Like a flower planted where flowers aren't supposed to grow, but growing anyway. It could get stomped on, but the roots are deep—it'll grow back no matter what you put it through. That's what she reminded me of as she walked around the room, completely unaware of me, just going through the motions. She'd smile at customers, but there was something so defeated in her dark gaze—like she was barely holding on. But still having a core strength that kept her from completely giving up.

Her fragile strength and the weight she seemed to carry on her delicate shoulders tugged at the protector in me—the defender.

I want to ease her burden, even if I don't know her.

But now I'm the reason she's in this mess. She finally saw me and the moment our gazes locked on each other, it was like everything else stopped. No chatter existed, and everything faded to black but her. My gut clenched like it does when I know I've made the right decision on the field even if it hasn't completely come to fruition yet.

It's how I knew I needed to talk to this woman. To get her name. Her number.

Her ring size.

I'm not usually so impulsive, but I want to know everything about her in a way that makes me question my sanity a little.

And I think the intensity of my gaze scared her like a rabbit noticing a wolf's gaze locked on it. I might not have caused her to run into that guy, but I might as well have since I was the reason she was running away.

But running away has never been in my nature, and I plan to help this woman however I can, starting with getting her job back so that haunted expression on her face will go away.

"Tony, was it?" I cut off her boss midsentence. I have no idea what he was saying, but his eyes brighten at my acknowledgment.

"Yes. Name whatever you'd like, Mr. Romero, and we'd be happy to accommodate you in order to fix this little snafu."

"Give this woman her job back."

Tony's jaw goes slack, and I can practically see him trying to figure out how to backtrack. My eyes squint as I watch him the way I would an opponent. He shoots a glare at her—I hate that I still don't know her name—and then looks at me as if he'd never done it. Men that smooth are usually snakes in my experience.

I don't have time for snakes.

"That's not a difficult request, is it?" I add when he continues to flounder with a response. A simple okay would suffice.

He grabs my arm and moves like he wants to turn us away from her and talk privately, but I stand firm, unyielding. This twig of a man isn't moving me anywhere without my say-so. I stare down at him, channeling my most intimidating expression, and his confident demeanor falters.

"Listen, I think it's great that you want to defend her, but she's a shit waitress and I was going to fire her anyway." He doesn't even have the decency to lower his voice so she won't hear him. Prick. "But what else could I do for you?"

What an asshole.

"Nothing," I grumble, not trusting myself not to say something worse and make this situation infinitely more complicated than it already is.

Tony shrugs and slaps my back like we're the best of

buds. "Well, just come find me if you think of something, and I'll be happy to take care of you." And then he walks away back to the bar, with not a single glance to the woman he's just obviously devastated.

The woman watches him until he gets behind the bar and starts talking to the bartender. The next singer is announced, and when the deep voice booms into the audience, she jumps a little. Then, as if snapping out of a trance, she moves swiftly toward a door labeled "employees only."

Like a puppy, I follow her.

I stop outside the door and decide to wait, because I'm not a creep, even if I kind of feel like I've lost my mind a little bit. It's not long before she comes blasting out the door, her face stormy and unseeing of anything besides her path to the front door.

"Hey, um...Miss." She doesn't acknowledge me so I walk a little faster. My strides are much longer than hers, but she's walking so fast, I still have to move quickly. My fingers itch to reach out and stop her, but I keep seeing her haunted face when Tony fired her, and I don't know how she'd react to being touched by a stranger. I have no desire to make her uncomfortable—or worse, afraid of me.

I'm aware of my size and how intimidating I can be. Especially for a woman as petite as she is.

Since she doesn't acknowledge my voice, I jog to reach her side and come up just slightly in front of her—not enough to stop her forward momentum, but enough that she can't miss me. Her steps stutter when her gaze falls on me.

"Hey, can I talk to you for a second?" I ask, trying to be as approachable as possible.

Her steps slow and then she stops, her dark brows nearly meeting when she scrunches up her face in suspicion. "Why?"

Before I can speak, she closes her eyes and lets out a sigh, holding her hand up to me in a stop gesture. "You know what, it doesn't matter. I'm not interested in a drink or a date or whatever mundane thing you're about to offer me. I don't know who you are, but you're clearly someone important, and knowing someone who gets a lot of attention is the last thing I want to do. Have a great life."

She turns to head out the door, and I know if she passes through that threshold, I'll have lost my chance forever.

"What about a job?"

# FIVE

# Danae

I couldn't have heard him right.

Did the sexy, mysterious stranger who actually came to my defense instead of being a misogynistic asshole like I'm painfully used to just offer me a job?

I spin on my heel and look at him with a healthy dose of skepticism. "A job?"

He swallows, his Adam's apple bobbing in a way that should not be so attractive. "Yeah."

"Doing what?"

He blinks twice like he can't believe I'm talking to him and didn't think we'd get this far in the conversation. There's no way this guy isn't used to women falling all over him. He's easily over six feet and all thick muscles. I'm not sure exactly what he does, but it wouldn't surprise me if he was an athlete in college. He's got bronze skin that is a shade darker than mine and brown eyes that remind me of the deep brown of an espresso bean. They gaze at me with such undisguised sincerity that it throws me off. I haven't met very many people in my life who didn't want something from me, and certainly not since I've been on the run.

"I need a housekeeper," he says quickly.

I continue staring at him, trying to figure out what his real play is. Most people can't stand the silence and will fill it by rambling. Hottie is no different.

"My house is too big for me to keep up with all the day-to-day stuff, especially during the season."

"You're an athlete?" I expected as much, but it's nice to have my suspicions confirmed.

He smiles, and I hate how much it warms my insides and makes me want to trust him. "Yes, ma'am. I'm a strong safety for the best team in the NFL."

"The Patriots?" I tease, having just come from Boston and knowing how die-hard everyone there was for the Pats.

He grabs his chest like I've physically wounded him. "You're trying to kill me. Please tell me you're not a Pats fan."

A reluctant smile pulls up the corners of my lips. "I'm not."

He looks up to the ceiling and puts his hands together in a praying gesture. "Thank God, or else I'd have to reconsider my offer." He grins at me, and it's charming to see how he smiles with his whole face, his eyes crinkling in the corners.

It takes me a second to realize I'm smiling wider, and I quickly school my expression and cross my arms over my chest. "What makes you think I'm any good at housekeeping?"

He shrugs. "I don't actually know. But I do know the bullshit with that guy wasn't your fault." He gestures over to where Tony fired me.

"What about what Tony said about me being a shit worker?"

"I think his actual words were that you were a shit waitress." He leans forward ever so slightly, but not enough to invade my space. "Fortunately, I don't need a waitress at my house." His smile is still teasing, but there's something about it that also makes me feel...safe.

I can't remember the last time I felt safe, and it's not a feeling I'm sure I'm ready to trust.

I don't smile or return his teasing. "What if I'm a shit housekeeper?"

"Then you can find something else and quit. Either way, I wouldn't just throw you out on the street."

I narrow my gaze at him. "Why are you trying to help me?" This is the real root of what I want to know. This guy doesn't know me from Adam.

His smile fades and his eyes seem to glow with an intensity that makes me catch my breath. "Because I hope someone would do the same if one of my sisters were in trouble. I don't know your story and I don't need to, but I know when someone needs help, and I'd like to offer whatever assistance I can. We can discuss pay and benefits if you'd like. I'm not trying to set you up for failure here or take advantage. I'm just trying to help."

I mostly believe him, but a part of me wishes I didn't. The other part still thinks he's holding something back. He's already made me feel seen in a way I've never felt before. Getting to know each other is a bad idea.

But...

I don't know if I have another choice. Tony stiffed me on my pay, so there's no way I can pay for any more nights at the motel I've been staying at—not if I want to eat too. I'm out of options.

Except for the one he's offered me.

"You don't even know my name," I say.

His smile grows wide and his brown eyes sparkle. "I was

just looking for an appropriate time to ask. I'm Gabe. Gabe Romero." He stretches out his hand for me to shake.

I tentatively place my hand in his, but try to maintain my unaffected demeanor. "Well, Gabe. Gabe Romero. I'm Danae."

It surprises me when my real first name is the one that slips out. It's been a long time since I've gone by Danae. Tony, my asshole boss, knew me as Diana.

"Danae..."

"Smith." My first name may be real, but my last name isn't. I doubt I'll ever tell him my real last name—Danae Badalyan. It pains me not to use it because it was my mother's last name and she was beyond proud of her Armenian heritage, but I would be too easy to find if I kept it. It's been a long time since anyone has called me by my birth name, but names like Smith and Jones are so much easier to hide under.

"When you say pay and benefits, what are we talking here?" I ask, still waiting for the bait and switch. I swear to God if this man suddenly suggests I sell him pictures of my feet or some other fetish, I'm going to lose my shit.

"I can offer you $2000 a week and you can live in the pool house. It's fully furnished as a mother-in-law suite, but my mom refused to live in it. She loves her house too much, so I just use it as the pool house."

My brain is still stuck on the two grand a week. I open and close my mouth like a fish desperate for water. "I'm s-sorry. Did you say two grand a *week*? Or did you mean two grand a month?" I've barely been scraping together two grand a *month*.

I've eaten so many peanut butter sandwiches, I'd be happy to never see them again.

He stares at me with concern. "Is that enough?"

Who the hell is this guy?

"How much did you pay your last housekeeper?"

He gets a sheepish look on his face and grips the back of his neck, which only pronounces his thick biceps. "I, uh, well, I've never had one actually. But I promise I'm good for the money." He gives me that smile that crinkles the corners of his eyes and endears him to me more every second.

Damn him.

"I believe you," I say, fighting back a gasp and counting figures in my head. Assuming I spend some on groceries and whatnot, I could build up a pretty hefty safety net just working for him for a month or two. Enough to get by a little more comfortably the next time I have to move.

"I also live in a gated community," he says.

I'm not sure why he tacks that on. There's no way he could know it would be the ultimate selling point for me. I've never been able to live in a gated community, but that would ensure a level of security I'm desperate for.

"I know I've thrown this at you. I can give you time to think about it." His tone suggests giving me time is the last thing he really wants, but I don't ponder it too long. "I...I could give you my number to call me when you decide."

He looks around us and grabs a business card and pen off the nearby abandoned hostess stand. He turns it over and writes a number on it. When he's done, he stares at the card for a second before finally handing it to me.

"That's my personal cell."

I look down at the card and then back up at him. "You don't give out this number very often, do you?"

"No, I don't. And I'd appreciate it if you didn't post it online. It's hell getting a new number."

"I'm guessing this isn't your first one?"

He chuckles. "No. It's my third. I made some dumb

mistakes with women as a rookie and gave it out like it was one of Oprah's Favorite Things."

"That's a weird reference for a guy to make," I say.

He shrugs again like he's heard that before. "I have a mom, two sisters, and lots of *tias*—aunts. I know way more about girly shit than I'd care to admit."

It's this brief tidbit of honesty and the way he gets bashful about his rookie mistakes that tips me over the edge. Since leaving Mitch, I've followed my gut and it's kept me alive so far. Maybe I've officially lost my mind this time to agree to move in with a complete stranger, but I can't turn down an opportunity to shore up a little nest egg and feel safe.

"Alright. I'll do it."

His eyes widen in shock. "You will?"

"When can I move in and begin work?" I need to get started saving as soon as possible. I've already been in LA for three weeks, and time is ticking before Mitch inevitably finds me.

"Uh, I mean, you could move in tonight. Wait, no. That's dumb. I'm sure you have to pack and shit—"

"I don't have to pack. Tonight works."

His curious gaze searches mine for an answer to an unspoken question I'm not ready to give him. But the truth is, I never leave anything behind at the motel. I learned my lesson after my stuff got ransacked when I briefly lived at a cheap motel in New York. Now, I always keep everything essential in my backpack that goes with me wherever I go.

"Alright. Then do you want to follow me?"

I wince. He assumes I have a car when I've been taking the bus to get everywhere. Cars are expensive to maintain and don't serve me well when I have to up and move at a moment's notice. I had one briefly in Boston—but that was a spare the owners of the house said I could use.

"Actually, you mind if I get a ride with you? I don't have my own car."

"Sure," he says, seeming pleased. "I just didn't want to make any assumptions."

I nod but don't say anything else.

"Are you ready to go now?"

"Ready as I'll ever be."

# SIX

# Gabe

*What the fuck am I doing?* is the first thought I have as I enter my house with Danae at my heels. The second thought hits me only a moment later.

*My mom and sisters are never going to let me live this down.*

I promised them after a particularly embarrassing tabloid fiasco with Dom a year ago that I was done making stupid decisions. And yet, despite how stupid this might appear on the surface—I'm essentially inviting a stranger into my house to rob me blind or take advantage of my generosity in ways I could never even comprehend—it doesn't *feel* stupid.

It feels right.

But that might just be me, because I don't think Danae's guard could get any higher. Her gaze darts around my house —clocking entrances and exits, windows, and the layout— and, not for the first time, I wonder what her story is. She's definitely spooked, but she didn't hesitate to speak her mind when I offered her this job, which makes me think she's definitely got some grit inside of her. It makes me admire her even though I don't know anything about her.

I give her a tour of the inside of my house—my relatively clean house. My mom didn't raise a slouch, and she'd skin me alive if I didn't pick up after myself, even in my own home. She ingrained in me the work ethic that has driven me to be the success that I am, and it's carried over in all aspects of my life.

Well, maybe not all, but most.

Once I've shown her the main house, we head out to my backyard overlooking the city in the distance. The landscaper who designed the yard planted lush foliage that gives a sense of privacy, almost like I'm in my own personal oasis. I can see the world, but no one can see me. It's my happy place, my Zen garden where I can recharge and disconnect from the craziness that can sometimes be my life. It's a big reason why I've never thrown any parties here or invited women over. I didn't want it sullied.

To be fair, it was our QB, Jack, who first gave me the idea. He said his wife, Paige, was the first woman he ever brought to his house, and I loved the idea.

I wonder what it means that I didn't even hesitate to offer it to Danae.

I knew there was something about her that called to me back at the bar, but I never could've imagined it'd be so strong that I would break one of my golden rules. What other rules would I break for this woman?

"Well, this is the pool house," I say, entering the small building nestled against the side of my property and facing the pool. "There's a bedroom, full bath, and small kitchenette. Make yourself at home. You can text me if you need anything, or call me. Oh! There's also an intercom system that's wired to the house so you just press this button," I say, moving toward the small box next to the door. "And you'll be able to reach me in the main house."

She nods her head and watches me with a bemused look on her face. Her eye makeup is smudged, and I wonder if she did it on purpose in an attempt to hide how mesmerizing her brown eyes are, but it's not working. I want her to keep staring at me like she is now, even if I suspect it's at my own expense.

"Do you not have a lot of guests?" she asks.

"Just my mom and sisters usually."

"Your dad doesn't come over?"

A familiar tightness squeezes my throat. "Ah, no. He passed away when I was thirteen from cancer."

Her face morphs with mortification. "Oh God, I'm so sorry."

"It's okay. You didn't know."

She chews her bottom lip like this small insight into my personal life has made her more curious about me, but I know she won't ask me what she wants to know. I suspect it's a protective mechanism to make sure no one turns the tables on her to pry into her life.

"Well..." I say, breaking the awkward silence that's ensued. "I'll let you get settled and get some sleep. Good night."

I open the door and I'm about to step out when I hear a quiet "good night" and my feet practically float all the way back to my house.

When I enter and my gaze scans my surroundings, I'm brought painfully back to earth. I'm not a messy guy. There's a reason I haven't needed a housekeeper. What the hell am I going to have her do here?

I pull my phone out of my pocket and dial the most

responsible guy I know. Romel answers on the fourth ring. "Hey man, what's up?"

"You got a minute?" I ask.

"Yeah, sure. It'll give me an excuse to procrastinate picking up after Kaylee. How is it possible for such a tiny person to create such a giant mess?"

"Dude, you're asking the wrong guy."

Maybe I should ask Danae if she wants to work for Romel. As soon as the idea comes into my head, I immediately banish it. No. I want her here.

"I've got a bit of a situation," I start.

"Were you out with Dom?" Romel asks.

"No."

"Okay, color me intrigued." I'm not surprised his first instinct was that Dom was responsible for getting me into a mess; that's usually what happens when you hang out with him.

"I met a girl—a woman—at Emma's open mic thing tonight." I hesitate, and it's long enough that he responds.

"Okay," he drags out. "It's been a while since you've dated anyone, or even hooked up with a woman, so putting yourself out there is a good thing. I'm not seeing the problem."

I reach up and grip my neck, knowing this next part is going to make him question my sanity—but no more than I've questioned it multiple times tonight. "I invited her to work for me as my housekeeper and live in my pool house."

Silence.

"Romel?"

"You did what?" There's no denying the complete disbelief in his voice.

"Please don't make me repeat it. I already feel a little crazy."

"A little?! You just invited this woman to live with you? She could be press! Think about what happened to Matt with that reporter that was trying to get dirt on Jack and Paige. Or worse, she's trying to trick you into knocking her up and having a free ride for the next eighteen years."

"She's not like that. And she's not a reporter."

"How do you know? You just flipping met her!" I roll my eyes at his kid-friendly cursing. If ever there was a time to use the actual f-word, now is it. I can practically hear him rolling his eyes and shaking his head on the other end of the line. "You, Dom, and Ty are going to drive me to an early grave from your dumbass mistakes," he mumbles.

"What if it's not a mistake?"

That makes him pause. "You said you hired her as your housekeeper."

"Yeah."

"You're the cleanest guy I know. I'm pretty sure Mr. Clean couldn't do a better job."

I rub my hand over my face. "Yeah, that's kind of my problem. I don't know what work to give her."

"Why did you hire her then?"

"Because I'm part of the reason she got fired. And—"

"Okay, hold up. Got her fired? So, this wasn't just a girl out with her friends? This was a waitress?"

"Yeah."

"And how exactly were you responsible for her being fired?"

"It's complicated."

"Uncomplicate it for me."

I sigh heavily. How do I explain what I felt when I first saw her? How do I put into words the way my body sparked to life like I'd been living in stasis until her gaze connected with mine? And how do I confess any of this without sounding like a chump?

"I don't know if this will make any sense, but there was something about her. From the moment I saw her, I was drawn to her in a way I've never been drawn to anyone. And I think she might've felt something too and it spooked her. She ran into another customer, spilling drinks all over him, and her boss fired her. At that point, all I wanted to do was fix it because it felt like that might be the straw that broke the camel's back for her, and I couldn't stand to play a part in her breaking."

"What do you mean?" There's only curiosity in his tone—none of the judgment I expected.

I sit down heavily on my white couch, staring out to the backyard and the city lights beyond. I see her silhouette move behind the sheer curtains before the lights in the pool house go off, and all that's left behind is darkness.

"She seemed haunted, and like losing her job might break her, but I'm telling you, man, this woman has a core of steel in her—I can tell. I didn't want to see her broken, so I offered her what I could think of that might help her catch a break."

"I'm worried that this is when your need to protect people is finally going to backfire on you," he confesses, and it feels like he's squeezing my heart.

"Well, that's a risk I'm going to take. I'm not gonna kick her out now. What kind of heartless bastard would I be then?" Not to mention, I'm not sure I could do it simply because the idea of never seeing her again makes me feel empty and cold in a way I've never felt before.

"Fair enough," he says. "So what do you need from me?"

"What do I have her do here?"

"Well, you need to clearly lay out her responsibilities as your employee. Maybe write something up with everything laid out including her pay and all that. Maybe walk in some mud or something, so your house is actually dirty."

I laugh. "Shut up. You're just jealous."

"Wait until you have kids, Gabe, and then come talk to me about how easy it is to keep a clean house. Hell, send her my way and she'll be constantly cleaning. I love Kay more than life itself, but I don't know how that kid always manages to get everything she touches sticky. How does that even happen?"

He sounds completely perplexed, but he has no idea how much I crave having kids of my own. My immediate family wasn't huge, but with three kids and lots of extended family, there was always a lot of noise and laughter. I want that. But as it stands now, this house is painfully quiet.

And yet...the stark emptiness I've been feeling isn't as prominent as it was when I left my house to go to hear Emma sing tonight, and I can only attribute that to one change—the mysterious beauty now living in my pool house.

SEVEN

# Danae

I don't understand why Gabe hired me.

Like, at all.

Despite how huge his house is, it's not even all that dusty, and it's certainly not dirty. There are no socks lying around or stinky gym shorts. I dated a jock briefly in high school, and I remember his car smelled like a locker room and a dumpster had a baby. It was disgusting.

Gabe, on the other hand, is so clean that his house looks magazine worthy all the time.

When I took this job, I was prepared to be cleaning constantly from sunup to sundown. I figured there'd be endless tasks to do that could keep my mind and body occupied, especially for two grand a week. In the week I've been working for him, though, I've struggled to find things to do. I wipe down already spotless counters. I scrub already clean floors, and dust things before dust has even had a chance to accumulate.

My own place isn't even this tidy.

Wait—no. *His* place. The pool house isn't mine. I'm just borrowing it temporarily.

I shake my head and move toward a room I haven't spent much time in. When I was first getting the lay of the house, I noticed that this room seemed to be used for storage, so I've not bothered with it. But now that I have nothing else to do and I'm desperate to find work that actually makes this job feel like a job, I decide to check to see if any of the boxes are labeled and need to be sorted.

When I enter the room, I take stock of the big, brown cardboard boxes. There are about ten spread around the space that's fairly small compared to other rooms in the house, but still large. Gabe has several rooms that are as empty as this one, which makes me wonder how long he's lived here. The window looks out to the pool, and I glance down to see Gabe still doing his laps. He's been out there for at least half an hour, and I've avoided watching him, but now that I've seen him, the temptation to stare is too great to resist. His strong arms sweep through the water in smooth strokes, his large body moving with grace and precision. When he reaches the end of the pool, he flips and pushes off the wall, flying through the water toward the other side.

I stare, unable to look away, as he does two more laps and then braces his hands on the side of the pool and pushes himself up and out of the water. My breath catches and a bolt of lust hits me so unexpectedly that I have to grab the windowsill to steady myself. Water drips down his light-brown skin in rivulets, and a silver chain with a crucifix glistens as it's hit by the sunlight. My mouth waters with the desire to lick every wet drop off his body.

*What the hell is wrong with me?*

I spin away from the window and lean my back against the wall, taking a deep, shaky inhale. It's been so long since I've been turned on that it takes me a moment to get control of my body.

Gabe is attractive. I can admit that. But I can't let it go further than that. I'm on the run and in no position to develop a stupid crush on a man like Gabe—a man with wealth, power, and fame rivaling that of the man I've been running from.

Gabe could destroy me with a snap of his fingers.

I refuse to give another man that kind of power over me.

I let that thought settle in my mind and move down my body until it feels like I'm coated with invisible armor. With one more inhale and exhale, I move back to the reason I came into this room to begin with. Most of the boxes are labeled, so I start organizing them by room. Then I start opening them to double-check the contents. One box doesn't have a label, so I open it first to figure out where I should put it and am surprised to find it filled with comic books. Hundreds of comic books.

I delicately pull one out and look it over. It's a Marvel comic, and I flip through the pages admiring the artistry. I've never really read one before, but I can appreciate how the graphics enhance the story. It's impressive how well comics and graphic novels can tell so much with so few words simply by relying heavily on the visuals. I wonder if this is where the phrase "a picture is worth a thousand words" came from.

I get lost in the story, until the clearing of a throat startles me and I snap the comic book shut. I can feel my cheeks heat, but I'm grateful my complexion hides most of my blush.

Gabe leans against the door frame, one leg crossed over the other and his hands tucked in his pants. There's a warmth in his eyes that doesn't fade as his gaze darts to the box of comics, but a slash of pain shoots across his face before quickly disappearing. He pushes off the doorjamb and walks over to me.

He's so big, my heart starts to race—a mix of fear and anticipation. I hate that I'm still a little afraid of him. He's been nothing but kind to me, but my body and mind can't forget that I trusted someone else who convinced me he was kind and caused me the worst pain of my life. While Gabe doesn't seem anything like Mitch, I still can't quite let my guard down with him.

I'm not sure what it says about me that after only a week, a small part of me wants to open up to him.

But trusting someone is dangerous.

He sits down on the floor and crosses his legs as he peeks into the box. He reminds me of a little kid finding an old box of toys, but there's a lingering tightness around his eyes, evidence of that flash of pain I saw just a moment ago.

"I forgot these were in here," he says softly, his fingers delicately picking up the next comic in the stack.

"Seems like you were really into comics," I say, and immediately the words feel lame. I shouldn't have said anything at all.

But Gabe doesn't seem to notice my cringe, his gaze still on the comic in his hands. "My dad loved them growing up, and before I could even read, he'd read to me and we'd look at the pictures together. My earliest memories of him are of us sitting in his big lounge chair reading comic books together. He was a huge Marvel fan," he says, his voice tightening at the end as he glances up at me. The pain in his eyes is crystal clear now and he doesn't bother to hide it away like before.

"You miss him," I say so softly it's almost a whisper.

He nods. "I love my mom and sisters, but it's hard to grow up as the only boy without your dad. He was my hero, and losing him..." His voice cracks and he looks back down at the comic—I suspect to hide the tears that were welling in his eyes. After a minute, he clears his throat and says, "Losing him was hard on us all in a lot of different ways, but I felt this pressure to be the man of the house, to step up in a way I never had to. It was on me to take care of my mom and sisters and make sure they were protected."

He says this like it was an honor, but that's a lot of pressure on a thirteen-year-old.

He continues, still not looking at me. "All I wanted was to make my dad proud of me, even if he wasn't here. I wanted him to know he raised an honorable son who could be his legacy."

His words slice a crack in my armor as my heart aches for the little boy that Gabe used to be and the man he's become. Even if I don't know him well, I can tell he's exactly the kind of man he wanted to be. Or maybe that's the kind of man I want to believe he is.

"I'm sure he'd be proud of you," I say.

He glances up at me, his eyes slightly red from holding back his tears. "Thanks," he says, his deep voice gruff.

He gently places the comic back in the box. "Did your mom or dad ever get you into anything like this?" he asks, gesturing to the box.

There's a pinch in my chest, but the panic that usually rises when someone asks me something personal isn't there. I nibble the inside of my lip, unsure if I should open up to him or not. I know he was vulnerable with me just now, but what if it's a trap?

Can I really afford to take that risk?

I've kept everyone at arm's length for so long, it feels foreign to even consider letting him know me, even if it's just the smallest piece.

He watches me with an open expression, his body relaxed and a calm patience emanating from him. I might be making a huge mistake, but I can't help but want to share something with him.

"I love romance novels. My mom used to have stacks of old Harlequin romances, and I'd sneak them into my room when I was a teenager." I look down at my hands, my heart aching even as a smile tips my lips up. "I suspect she knew and left them out for me. Eventually, I stopped sneaking them and we'd share our favorites."

A hot tear slips and I quickly wipe it away, embarrassed by the rush of emotion. It's been so long since I've been able to talk about her with someone else. I miss her so much, and another silent tear tracks down my cheek.

"What happened to her?" he asks softly.

"She died in a car accident when I was eighteen." I will never forget getting the call and the way it felt like someone had ripped my whole world away from me.

"And your dad?"

I shake my head and brush away more tears, angry at myself for not being able to hold it together. I've been so strong for so long; I don't know why I'm failing now. "I never knew him."

We're both silent for a while, but it doesn't feel awkward or strained. It feels like he's giving me space to let my emotions run their course before I shove them back in the box deep inside me. Finally, I glance up, and I'm relieved to see him staring at the box holding memories of his father.

It doesn't feel like he was analyzing my grief, but like we were grieving our losses together. Like maybe by sitting together while we both mourned the loss of such integral people in our lives, it lessened the pain that's always there, even if only by a fraction.

He turns his head and looks at me, but this time it feels like it did that night at the bar—like he can see into my soul and every desire and fear I hide there.

"Thank you for sharing with me," he says, as if he truly understands how hard that was for me.

I can't speak over the lump in my throat, so instead I just nod and then stand up. I take a second to pull myself together and then leave the room with a lame excuse about needing to get back to work.

He lets me go without trying to stop me and I'm relieved, but only until I get back downstairs. And then a different kind of fear settles deep inside me.

Fear that this man is going to strip me of all my armor, and wondering what I will have left when he does.

The urge to run is strong, but I can't yet. I need the money from this job, and I can't deny that I feel safer in his house than I have in months—years even.

No, I just need to make sure we don't share a moment like that again.

I'm not sure I'll survive it.

EIGHT

# Gabe

Music pumps through my Bose headphones as I twirl the small, bright-orange square in my hands. It's folded so the words are hidden, but I've had them memorized since I first read it.

*Good luck at your away game -D*

As if this woman hasn't fucked with my head enough in the last three weeks, now she's all I can think about when I'm not on the field.

Our Post-it notes started as a way for me to talk to her without making her feel uneasy. I would leave her a thank you note, or a could-you-do-this-today note, instead of talking to her. And maybe that was the coward's way out, but it felt like the best course of action after our conversation about my dad and her mom. She seemed more determined to shut me out after that, so I needed a way to let her know I wasn't a threat to her. A way to still stay close without scaring her any more than she already was.

At first the notes were all one-sided, and I told myself I

was fine with that—even if I craved some kind of response from her. I could still hear the soft cadence of her voice as she spoke about her mom and their shared love of romance novels. The way her chestnut-brown eyes lit up and the corners of her lips curled with a smile that made my chest feel light. But she'd barely said a word to me since that day, and every day that my Post-it notes disappeared without a response, I wished more and more that I could find some way to connect with her—to get her to open up to me. Then one night, I came home after a game and was starving. When I opened the fridge, I found a container with lasagna and a bright-blue sticky note on top. *I made too much. Help yourself.*

I'm pretty sure the joy I felt in that moment could've powered a dozen small countries.

Since then, the notes have gone back and forth, some mundane, and others friendly.

I've kept every single one from her.

None of them ever veer into flirty—and fuck, do I spend a ridiculous amount of time making sure none of mine cross that line and set me back with her—but they've shown me a different side of her than the scared, yet tough woman I met at the bar that first night.

She's considerate in the way she seems to have picked up on my schedule and leaves notes like the one I hold in my hand, generous with how she always makes extra food for me when she's cooking, and funny which she's slowly revealed with simple teasing or sticky notes with jokes that I never would've expected from her, and that never fail to make me laugh.

With each note, I feel like she lets down her guard ever so slightly. And worse, each one makes me want to know every single piece of her even more than before.

The orange sticky note folded in fourths is slightly frayed from how many times I've held it this weekend, like a fucking talisman reminding me each time I touch it of the woman in my house.

Ty sits down next to me on the plane back to LA and glances at the slip of paper in my hand, his brows slightly furrowed. "Okay, I gotta ask. What's with the paper? You've pulled that thing out so many times this weekend, you'd think it was your good luck charm."

"Maybe it is," I say, watching it twist in my fingers. "We did win, after all."

"Come on man, what's going on with you?"

I look over at him. "Do you think it's possible to fall for someone through Post-it notes?"

Ty's dark-blond eyebrows shoot up to his matching hairline. "You're seeing someone?"

"No," I say, my gaze moving back to the sticky note and wondering what Danae is doing right now. I left her my number again in case she needed anything, but she hasn't used it. I haven't seen her in three days, and it's disconcerting how much I miss her. Her quiet strength. The small smile she throws my way when I inevitably fumble my words trying to talk to her without making her uneasy. Everything about her.

For someone who's trying to fly under the radar, she has a presence, and her absence is felt as though I'm missing a limb, which seems insane given the state of our...whatever it is. Employer and employee seems too formal, but I don't know that we've veered into friendship yet.

And we're certainly a long way away from what I'd really like to be with her.

"I'm confused then," Ty says.

I slide the sticky note into my pocket with a heavy sigh. "Yeah, well, get in line."

"Huh," he says, leaning back in his chair, but looking at me with one arched eyebrow and amusement shining in his blue eyes.

"What?"

"Just didn't know if I'd ever see the day when you'd be pussy-whipped."

Rage licks hot in my belly, and I clench my fists and fight the urge to clock him for diminishing Danae to something so base. "I'm not," I say between clenched teeth.

His eyes narrow as he catalogs my reaction. "You sure about that?"

"Yeah, I'm fucking sure." I turn toward the window, effectively ending the conversation.

"Tell me more about this mystery Post-it note woman."

Okay, or maybe not.

Facing him again, I say, "You know, you used to be better about reading people's body language."

He tips his head back and lets out a deep laugh. "Oh, man. I'm still good at reading body language. I'm just choosing to ignore yours because I know you well enough to know you need to talk it out. So talk."

"Nothin' to talk about."

"I call bullshit."

"Call bullshit all you want. It doesn't change the truth, so there's nothing to talk about."

"Come on, if I'd let some woman move in with me and gave her a job, you know you'd be all over me. I've given you three weeks to 'fess up. So spill."

Spinning in my seat, I turn to the seats behind us where Romel and Dom are sitting—Dom's got his headphones on and is passed out, while Romel is watching a movie on his tablet. My movement causes him to glance up at me, and he pulls his earbuds out.

"What?"

Pointing my thumb at Ty, I say, "You told him?"

"You mean about your horrible lapse of judgment? Yeah, I told him. I was worried it might be an early sign of CTE or something serious."

My entire face goes slack. "That's not even funny."

He arches a brow. "Was I laughing on the phone that night when you called me in a panic? No. I assume by the fact that you haven't said anything and your name isn't plastered all over the news, that things are going fine so far."

Ty readjusts in his seat so both of us are facing Romel and leaning over our chairs. I give up trying to keep it all to myself. These guys are the closest thing I have to brothers. If I can't tell them, who can I tell?

"They're going alright, but I wish she'd let me in a little more. I...I'm trying to be careful with her because she always seems on the edge of spooking, like some kind of timid horse or something. But it feels impossible to make forward momentum with that approach."

Ty frowns. "Why do you think she'd be spooked?"

"I don't really know. I mean, she hasn't told me much about herself, but there's this look in her eyes sometimes, like she's haunted by something."

"You think she's hiding something?" Ty asks.

"Well, that would make sense," Romel says before I get a chance to respond. "I mean, who the hell takes a job and moves in with a complete stranger the same night they meet?"

Ty shrugs. "Maybe she knew a good offer and didn't want to pass it up."

"Or, more likely, she's desperate and running from

something." Romel focuses on me. "Has any of your stuff gone missing?"

I clench my jaw, fighting down the anger boiling in my gut at how easily he judges her when he's never even met her. "No. She wouldn't do that."

"Man, I love you like a brother, but you don't know this woman, so you couldn't possibly know what she would or wouldn't do. For all you know, she could be doing a long con. I mean, come on, Gabe, are you really that naive?"

"Fuck you. Just because you're jaded about life, doesn't mean the rest of us have to be." I know I've gone too far as soon as the words leave my mouth, but there's no way to take them back now. Romel's face shutters and his teeth grind together while he stares hard at me.

"Forgive me for looking out for my friend," he grits out.

Ty, ever the peacemaker, glances between the two of us and then switches the focus of the conversation.

"You said you wished she'd open up with you. What is it exactly that you want with her?" Ty asks.

"You're going to think I'm certifiable," I say.

Romel scoffs, but his voice has lost the hard edge it held only moments ago, and I know we're going to be okay. "My brother, that ship has sailed. Now tell us more."

With a sigh, I explain. "I've never had to work so hard to earn someone's trust before, and I worry that any misstep will set me back big-time. I'm not usually so awkward with women, but when it comes to Danae, I'm a little out of my element."

"Well, what have you tried?" Ty asks, then glances down at my pocket where I shoved the sticky note. "Because if it's just passing sticky notes, that's middle school stuff and you really need to step up your game."

"I'm not trying to play a game at all. She's different than

any other woman I've been interested in, and I suspect she's been burned pretty badly in the past. I just want her to trust me. I don't know how to convince her that she can let her guard down with me—that I won't take advantage of her."

"Unfortunately, Gabe, all you can do is be yourself. The rest is up to her," Ty says.

"He's right," Romel adds. "We can't change people's past experiences to fit our agenda or hoped-for outcomes. I know that's probably not what you want to hear, but if you really like this girl and want something more with her, then just keep being you. Build that foundation and see where it leads. It may work out, but you also need to accept that it may not." He doesn't add that he still has doubts about her, but he doesn't need to. There's a hesitancy in his eyes, but I know after I snapped at him, he won't bring it up again.

Their advice isn't really what I want to hear—I was hoping more for a solid game plan that I could use like I would on the field—but I know they're right.

All I can do is give her time and prove to her with my actions that I'm worth letting in.

Unfortunately, I get the feeling time is not on my side.

When I get home that night, the house is dark, and I try to ignore the disappointment that I won't get to see Danae until tomorrow. I put my stuff down by the stairs and then move to the kitchen to get some water. As soon as I flick the light on, I see a pink sticky note sitting on the counter.

*Great game! There's some food in the fridge.*
*Goodnight, D.*

I smile, and whatever disappointment I felt fades as I grab a water bottle from the fridge and head out to the patio.

My body feels lighter than it has in days as I stare up at the stars. Joy and hope mingle together, keeping the smile on my face, only to be replaced by fear and a spike of adrenaline moments later when a scream pierces the air from the pool house.

Danae!

NINE

# Danae

The blackness feels heavy and suffocating as Mitch's voice taunts me from the shadows. My body jerks from his invisible punches, remembering all too well how it felt in real life. My heart races as panic grips my throat in a chokehold, trapping the scream that could save me from this hell.

A soft touch breaks through my subconscious, and it's almost more unsettling than reliving the abuse. A voice calls to me, but it's muffled by the panic causing a whooshing in my ears. Another gentle touch to my shoulder, and a more urgent call of my name. The shadows lift slowly at first and then all at once as I shoot up, nearly bumping heads with Gabe, who's leaning over me with a look of concern on his normally carefree face.

He reaches a hand out, and instinct takes over. I slide back to the headboard, curling my legs up underneath me and wrapping my arms around my body protectively as if that alone could protect me from this giant of a man.

I wince at the flash of hurt in his gaze, but my heart is still too panicked and the dream too fresh to reassure him that he shouldn't take this personally. Instead of towering over me and telling me it's okay like I expect him to, he gets down on his knees, his hands flat on the bed where I can see them and his body language screaming that he's no threat to me. He exaggerates his breathing, looking at me like I should mimic him, so I do—inhaling, then slowly exhaling.

We watch each other for several minutes before I realize that my heart has calmed and my palms are no longer sweaty. I stretch my legs out, letting the tension start to ease out of my tight muscles. My chest rises and falls with ease, and with it comes the exhaustion.

This is the fifth nightmare I've had in as many nights, and the lack of sleep is finally getting to me. But before I can attempt to sleep again, I need to deal with Gabe and the inevitable questions he must have.

My gaze drops to my lap.

"Go ahead and ask me," I say, resigned but still guarded. I'll tell him the bare minimum to get him to leave it alone. Then we can go back to...well, whatever we are. I'm not entirely sure where we stand, to be honest. Gabe isn't like any other guy I've met before. He's like the eye of a hurricane. He's this complete calm, but also a fierce defender who can twist your world completely upside down.

"What do you want to tell me?"

My gaze shoots to his, and my heart rate picks up in a way that's different from the fear that Mitch induces. But I can't even be surprised that he'd phrase the question like this—not about what he wants to know, but what I'm willing to tell him. It's this kind of thing that's put me so at ease with him in a way that terrifies me.

He makes me want to trust him.

But trust isn't something that comes easily to me. Not before Mitch and certainly not after.

I nibble my lip and then fight against the knot in my

stomach as I choke out, "What if I don't want to tell you anything?"

Once again, his eyes flicker with the briefest hint of hurt, and if I wasn't watching him so closely, I might've missed it. But when he speaks, his voice is still calm and soothing, accepting even. "Then you don't have to. Do you need anything? Water? I can run you a warm bath and then leave you alone."

"Can I ask you a question?"

"Of course," he says, as if the idea of me having to ask at all is ridiculous. As if he's an open book, which I guess he kind of is.

"What are you even doing in here?"

For the first time, he looks a little embarrassed, and his eyes drop to the blanket before he looks back up at me. "I..." He sits back on his heels, making him even smaller, and he huffs out a resigned sigh. "I like astronomy, and there was supposed to be a cool meteor shower tonight that I wanted to check out as soon as I got home. I was coming out to make sure it was clear enough to see it, and I heard you scream. I knocked but you didn't answer. I'm sorry for invading your privacy, but I was worried." He tacks on those last few sentences in a rush as if I'm going to chew him out for saving me from my own mind.

I didn't even realize I'd screamed, but now that he mentions it, my throat feels hoarse. In my nightmare, I hadn't been able to scream, though I'd certainly tried multiple times.

"It's okay," I mumble, my voice scratchy and raw—more from the emotions I'm battling than the aftereffects of my scream. "Thank you," I add.

We're both silent for long enough that it becomes awkward. He must feel it too because he clears his throat and then pushes himself up to standing, stepping away as soon as he's upright, and I appreciate the space he's giving me. He leaves my room, and a minute later, I hear the door of the pool house click shut. I lie back on the bed, staring up at the ceiling, wider awake than I think I've been in my entire life.

I close my eyes, hoping that if I just lie here with them closed, sleep will find me, but as soon as they're closed, I feel the familiar twist of panic in my chest from the darkness, from the nightmare that's still fresh in my mind.

Flinging the sheets off my body, I get up and walk to the bathroom, but stop as I pass the window. My gaze catches on the sight of Gabe lying flat on his back on a lounge chair, staring up at the sky.

Instead of going to the bathroom, I go to my closet and grab a sweatshirt and then head outside. He lifts his head when I open the door.

"Mind if I join you?"

He stares at me for a second like he's not sure if I really asked that and then says in a rush, "Not at all."

He sits up and adjusts the lounge chair next to his so it lies flat and then lies back down on his. I copy his position and fold my hands over my stomach as I stare up at the murky Los Angeles sky.

"I'm surprised you can see anything with all the light pollution."

He laughs and it's such a nice, carefree, deep sound that it fills my whole body with warmth. "Yeah. We'd be able to see it better if we drove out where it's darker, but since I just got home, I didn't really feel like leaving again, so I figured I'd just lie here and see what I can see."

I hesitate to ask the question that's on the tip of my

tongue. If I ask him, it opens up the door for him to ask me something. Am I ready for that?

I want to be. Maybe that's enough.

"What got you into astronomy?" I ask, looking at his profile—his strong jaw and nose that has a subtle bump like it was broken once and didn't heal correctly.

He turns his head to look at me, his eyes darting between mine like he's searching for more meaning in my question. Does he know how hard it was for me to ask it? How exposed I feel as I sit here waiting for him to answer and then inevitably turn the tables on me?

"Truth?"

"Always," I say, my voice a soft murmur.

He gets a bashful look on his face. "A girl I had the hots for in college liked astronomy. I got into it to impress her, but she ended up going for a guy who was on track to be a doctor."

He turns his head to look back at the stars, but there was something akin to inadequacy in his eyes, and I wonder what else transpired with that girl that made him get that look.

"I didn't get the girl, but I got a pretty cool hobby that I can enjoy anywhere I travel to." He looks back at me and shoots me a self-deprecating smirk. "I'm kind of a giant nerd if you haven't figured that out by now."

"Liking comic books and stars makes you a nerd?"

He laughs, and like always, the sound sends a warmth through my body. "That's only the tip of the iceberg. Stick around long enough and I'm sure you'll see me in all my nerdy glory."

My heart squeezes in my chest with the desire to stay long enough to see that part of him. I want to get to know him more than I've wanted to know anyone in years.

But what would he think if he knew me? *Really* knew me.

What happens when Mitch inevitably finds me and I have to move along again?

My gut twists at the idea of leaving Gabe. It's only been three weeks, but I feel more at home here than I've felt since my mom died.

Silence descends as we both direct our attention up, watching the occasional star that burns in an arc across the sky. I wait for him to ask me something personal, but he never does. Peace settles over me, burrowing deep into my bones until I'm relaxed and at ease on the lounge chair, lying in companionable silence with this man who came into my life and has given me a home and safety. I want to let my walls down, let him in. And maybe soon, I'll actually be able to.

"Gabe?"

"Yeah?"

"Thank you for coming to check on me," I whisper, feeling vulnerable but safe.

His deep, soothing voice lowers my guard even further as he whispers back, "Anytime, Danae. Anytime."

# Gabe

Lush lips brush across the tip of my cock before her pink tongue slides along the velvety flesh underneath the head. I shudder as pleasure ripples through my body and my fingers grip her hair.

"Let me taste you," I whisper, not demanding because I want this to be about her giving, not me taking.

She hums and my balls draw tight. She lifts up and starts to lie on her back, but I stop her with a gentle tug on her wrist. "Sit on my face, gorgeous."

Her smile is coy and devoid of the usual defensiveness that always seems to be just under the surface. Instead of grabbing the headboard like I expect, she spins around, putting her delectable round ass right in my face. I can't help myself and take a small nibble that makes her squeal. She pushes back farther, and then her glistening pussy is right there just waiting for me to ravage. I wrap my arms around her thighs and pull her down until she's fully sitting on my face and then I eat my fill of her. Her hips rock as she grinds against my face, and she lets out a shuddering moan right before she leans forward and takes me in her mouth.

I lose the rhythm I'd started at the feel of her warm, wet mouth. Fuck, she feels unreal. I grip her hips tighter and go for the gold, sucking her clit into my mouth as the telltale signs of my own impending orgasm ramp up. She deep throats my cock and swallows at the same time that I shove a finger in her ass and suck hard on her clit, and her thighs shake as her orgasm hits her.

A blaring sound jolts me awake at the same time that my orgasm hits me, and my naked body shakes as my cock spurts a much-needed, and yet somehow inadequate release all over me and my sheets. My chest heaves as my eyes slowly blink open, and I reach over to turn off the blaring alarm on my phone.

I set it back down and scrub my hands over my face. Fuck, that dream felt so real. Lifting up my sheet, I stare down at the mess. I haven't had a wet dream since I was a teenager. I drop my head back to my pillow and try to calm down—my heart is still racing and my mind right along with it.

Well, there's no way I can let Danae wash these, despite the fact she's taken over doing all the laundry. I don't even want to imagine how the hell I'd explain away the obvious wet spot.

I use a clean corner of the sheet and wipe off my stomach and my still-sensitive dick before getting out of bed and throwing on some sweats. I roll the defiled sheets up in a ball and slowly open my bedroom door, listening carefully to figure out where in the house Danae might be. There's music playing faintly in the direction of the living room, which means she might be dusting or something. If I'm fast, I should be able to put these in the wash before she even hears me.

I race down the stairs as quietly as I can and release a

relieved sigh when I manage to get the wash started with no issues. Until I spin around to find Danae standing there with a basket full of towels.

She tilts her head, her gaze moving to the washer behind me before focusing back on me. "I could've run a load for you."

My stomach tightens as I stare at her, my mind remembering every vivid detail of the dream that brought me down here in the first place. She arches a brow, and it takes every ounce of restraint not to adjust my rapidly hardening dick, but that would likely only draw her attention there.

"Uh, yeah, I suppose you could have, but it's no big deal. I'm used to doing it myself."

"Okay," she says slowly, her expression a mix between curious and guarded.

We stand there staring at each other, neither of us saying a word or making an attempt to move. A tension seems to swirl and thicken between us the longer we stand here, until I lose enough of my self-control that my body moves forward one step. She doesn't back away, and I start to take another step when the doorbell rings and both of us freeze.

"Who the hell?" I mutter, frustrated about the interruption but also grateful because I almost crossed a line I know she's not ready for—she's still too closed off. I try to shake off our encounter as I rush to the door. When I open it to see the woman standing on the other side, my heart starts racing for a completely different reason.

"Mom," I say, trying to hide the surprise—and the panic since I haven't told her about Danae yet. "What are you doing here?"

Her eyes narrow when I don't immediately invite her in, but instead step outside and close the door behind me.

"*Mijito*, please don't tell me you brought some girl home that you're hiding away in there. If she's fit to bring home, then she's fit to meet your mamá."

I lean down and give her a kiss on the cheek that she takes with an endearing smile. "That's not at all true, mamá. I just..." I falter, not sure what to say, but completely unable to lie to my mom. One, she'd know, even if I was the best liar in the world, which I'm not even close to being. Two, she always taught me that lying is disrespectful, and the last thing I ever want to do is disrespect the woman who raised me to be the man I am.

But I also can't tell her the complete truth either, especially with my head already a mess of inappropriate thoughts about my houseguest. Which puts me in a bit of a pickle.

"I didn't want you to see the maid I hired," I confess quietly.

She stares at me, her gaze sharp, but not giving away what she's thinking. She's always been good at that, and I've often wondered if all moms have that look where they can see into your soul or if it's just mine.

"Are you embarrassed that you needed one, or that you have one? Because while I didn't raise you to not pick up after yourself, I also know you're busy. There's no sense in being ashamed to have help."

I grip the back of my neck, which is a sure sign I'm uncomfortable, but it's also a habit I've never been able to break. "I'm not ashamed. She's just skittish is all. I didn't want to bother her with company while she's working, especially unexpected company."

Her eyes linger on me like she knows I'm not telling her the whole story, but she doesn't pry further. "That's alright. I offered to come up to LA to pick up some things for your *prima's* quince and figured if you didn't have work obligations, we could go out to brunch."

My shoulders sag with relief. "Brunch sounds great. I'm starved. I'll drive."

She puts a hand up to stop me when I take a step toward my garage—planning to open it from the outside instead of going through the house and risking a run-in with Danae—and shakes her head while a bemused smile flits across her face.

"*Espérate mijo,* I think you need a shirt first, no? I know football players all like to show off your muscles, but going to brunch in only gray sweats is a bit extreme."

My cheeks heat and I give her the same smirk that always used to get me out of trouble. She huffs out a laugh and then shoos me away. "Go change. I'll be in my car when you're ready."

I drop another kiss to her cheek and then run inside to change.

# ELEVEN

# Danae

My heart gallops like a herd of wild horses as Gabe rushes past me out of the laundry room. I drop the basket of towels to the floor and lean back against the wall, catching my suddenly short breath.

What the hell was that?

What is it about Gabe that makes me feel so...secure? And why does it have to be such a turn-on? He is huge—all jacked muscles and a serious, brooding expression whenever I've walked into his entertainment room while he was watching game tape. The times I've watched him play on TV, he's been fierce—never hesitating to take down an opponent by any means necessary. By all accounts, I should be terrified of him, but I'm not. I'm not scared when he smiles at me and he gets little crinkles at the corners of his eyes, or when he watches me when I talk—even if it's not often—like every word I speak matters to him more than anything else.

No, I'm not afraid of him at all.

Instead, I've started to get a little tingle in my belly every time we're in the same room together. Although right now it's definitely lower than my stomach, in a part of my body I wasn't sure would ever feel pleasure again. But it's sitting up and taking notice of the beast of a man with a tender heart who just zipped out of the room like his ass was on fire.

Thank God for the doorbell or who knows what I would've done, or how close I would've let him get to me.

Pushing off the wall, I follow after him, picking up the dustrag I'd discarded earlier when I collected the basket of dirty towels. He's not at the door, so I move toward the large picture window that looks out over the front of his house. Gabe is standing on his front porch, towering over a petite woman with dark hair similar to his, who is definitely older but has aged in such a way that it's hard to tell exactly how old she is. She smiles up at Gabe, and the expression on her face is so similar that it makes it instantly clear who this woman is—Gabe's mom.

I watch Gabe talk to his mom while I pretend to dust a large plant, giving me the perfect view out the front where they're standing without them being able to see me. He talks easily with her, although I can't hear what he's saying, and she smiles at him with a knowing gleam in her eye that reminds me so much of my mom. She used to look at me like that when she knew I wasn't being completely open with her, but was going to let me get away with it anyway.

That warm, fuzzy feeling in my stomach turns into a tight pinch of pain, and the vision of Gabe and his mom blurs slightly. I blink away an errant tear at the memory of my mom, the way she'd place her hand on my cheek and call me her brave girl when I was having a tough time. God, I miss her so much. She was my best friend growing up—the two of us were a team. The minute she was stolen from me, my entire life changed, and I've been stuck in this cycle of one bad thing after another, always dealing with everything alone and never quite figuring out where I belong.

I miss her cooking, especially her *lahmajun*—the ultimate comfort food made from a recipe passed down from her mom. No matter how many times I've tried to make it like she did, it never tastes quite right. I miss the way she'd let me lay my head in her lap, and she'd brush my hair with her fingers while she let me vent or cry or just be—where I didn't have to be strong or weak or anything in between; I could just exist in peace.

There have been so many nights I've needed that gentle caress and reassurance from her, so many nights I've felt alone and lost without her. The last twenty months have only made that feeling infinitely worse.

Another tear slides free as Gabe's mom holds up her hand and says something to him that causes a cheeky smirk to cross his face before he drops a kiss to her cheek and turns around to come back inside.

I brush away the tears quickly and move away from the window, but can't escape from Gabe when he walks through the space and stops in his tracks at the sight of me.

"Hey, that was my mom. I'm going to go out for a bit and spend some time with her."

I swallow thickly as my gaze scans his naked torso before I catch what I'm doing and quickly meet his eyes. My cheeks heat from embarrassment as his mouth tilts up on one side, but then his eyes crinkle with concern and he takes a step toward me.

I retreat, but can't go far with the wall at my back. My movement is enough to stop him though.

He tilts his head ever so slightly. "Are you okay?"

I steel my spine and tilt my chin up, feeling my invisible armor click back into place. "I'm fine."

My voice doesn't betray my moment of weakness, and I'm grateful for the practice I've had over the years. But Gabe doesn't respond like others have. Most people are happy with hearing "fine" because it lets them off the hook from having to listen to someone else's problems. I should've known Gabe wouldn't be like everyone else. He hasn't been from the start.

"Why don't I believe you?" he says softly, his voice like a tender caress whispering that it's okay to be honest.

But I've already had one moment of weakness today. I won't have another.

I shrug. "I don't know, but shouldn't you hurry since your mom is waiting?"

He frowns, his dark brows slashing toward his nose, while his mesmerizing brown eyes attempt to see into my soul. My stomach clenches with a ripple of guilt at making this man unhappy, which is completely ridiculous since he's just a temporary fixture in my life, like everyone else.

No one ever stays.

Not even me.

A month from now, I doubt I'll be in LA anymore, and I'll just be part of some story he tells his friends. Our lives couldn't be more different if we tried.

"Do you want me to bring you back something?" he asks, his frown slowly dissolving into acceptance of the boundary I've set.

His kindness is going to be my downfall. "No, but thank you."

He continues watching me as he says, "Sure."

I arch my brow when he still doesn't make a move to go get dressed, and he finally rips his gaze away. I feel the loss instantly.

Pointing with his thumb toward the stairs, he says, "Well, I should, uh..."

"Yeah," I say, not letting him finish.

With a nod, he turns and hustles up the stairs. I sag against the wall and tip my head back, staring at his white ceiling and wondering how much longer I'll be able to hide from him. Because if there's one thing I can admit to myself, it's that each time he looks at me like he wants to see the darkest parts of my soul, my resolve to keep him at a distance crumbles a bit more.

# TWELVE

# Gabe

Danae's bent over as she digs through a bottom drawer in my kitchen, and my mouth turns into a desert. The words I came in here to speak immediately evaporate as my gaze soaks up every inch of her perfect ass. My heart pounds a little harder and then starts racing when I realize what the hell I'm doing and forcefully avert my gaze.

*Don't be a creep, jackass.*

I take a deep inhale, hoping the extra oxygen might help the blood that was all flowing south halt its course and revert back to my brain so I can think clearly around this woman. Movement in my periphery causes me to look back over, and a low groan nearly escapes when she turns around and her tight T-shirt has ridden up her torso enough to tease me with a hint of her toned stomach.

*Stop it.*

She sees me and startles, scooting back against the counter, one hand to her chest and her eyes wide, breath uneven. "Gabe. Shit. You scared me."

Like a switch being flipped, all my desire disappears in the light of her fear. The last thing I want to do is scare her. I suspect that at least one man has made her afraid on purpose, and it's my new mission to make her feel as safe with me as possible. Especially after the bits and pieces she murmured during that night she had a nightmare. I don't want to remind her of the men of her past, and I'm willing to do the work to earn her trust—no matter what it takes.

I want her to know not all guys are scumbags.

"Sorry. I should've made a noise or something."

She shakes her head before I even finish my sentence. "No, it's me. Sorry. Do you need something?"

I've practiced how to say this all morning—and all last night if I'm honest—but still I'm worried it's going to come out in a way that makes her uneasy.

"I was wondering if you wanted to take the day off and go to the zoo with me."

She blinks at me. "The zoo?"

God, this was a stupid idea. Glancing away, I start a hasty verbal retreat. "You know what, it was dumb. Never mind."

I turn around and get to the threshold of the kitchen when her voice hits me like a football to the head.

"Wait!"

I glance back at her. She seems slightly unsure, her bottom lip trapped between her teeth, but her eyes are earnest and eager. "I'd love to go the zoo."

I face her completely now. "You would?"

She nods and her lips tilt up into a smile. The way it eases the worry lines around her eyes nearly brings me to my knees. Danae is a beautiful woman, but when she smiles, she transforms into a damn goddess.

"I haven't been to a zoo since I was a kid."

I swallow hard, reining in the feelings I know won't be

returned and nod. "Great, then let me just grab my keys and we can go."

"Do you mind if I change first?"

My gaze slides unbidden down her body, taking in her tight T-shirt and her formfitting yoga pants. She looks good to me, but if she'd rather wear something else, I'm not going to stop her. I nod and she hurries out of the kitchen.

"Be back in a few."

I grew up with sisters, and in my experience a "few" usually meant at least a half an hour—an hour if it was for a boy—but true to her word, she's back in my kitchen in less than ten minutes.

She's changed into a different shirt that has a higher neckline and is looser around her torso and a pair of jeans that still show off her toned legs. She has a cross-body purse, but I have no intention of letting her pay for our outing today. It may not be a date, but I invited her and I know she's saving her money.

She peppers me with general questions on our drive to the LA Zoo, and I answer them openly. I'm an open book for her if it'll put her at ease and maybe encourage her to tell me a little bit about herself. I'm rewarded when she shares some of her own preferences—favorite color, music, movies, and such—without me even asking.

"Why the zoo?" she asks, once we get to the zoo and start walking around looking at the animals.

I glance over at her. "What do you mean?"

"Of all the places you could've gone on your day off, why'd you want to come to the zoo?"

I shrug. "It reminds me of being a kid, when there was no pressure on my shoulders. When my dad was still alive. I loved elephants, so my dad would take me so I could watch them feed and care for the elephants. I grew up in San

Diego, which has a conservation zoo, so all the animals there are endangered or need rehabilitation of some kind. I loved those days when it was just me and him. After he died, I couldn't go to the zoo for a long time.

"In college, a girl I was dating wanted to go to the local zoo to see the new baby giraffe. I felt nauseous the whole way there, but as we entered the zoo and started walking around, I didn't think about my dad dying, or all the pain that came after. Instead, I remembered riding around on his shoulders making elephant sounds and laughing with him. I felt closer to him at a random zoo thousands of miles away from where I grew up than I had since he died. So now whenever I feel like I need a reset, I go to the zoo, and I remind myself about the kind of man my father wanted me to be."

When I glance over at her, her gaze is already on me, watching me with a carefully composed expression, all her emotions hidden away. Then, in a blink, her gaze softens. "I think he'd be really proud of the man you've become." Her words are quiet, but they hit me with a force I've only ever felt on the field.

"Thanks," I choke out over the emotion building in my throat.

We walk silently for a few minutes, looking at the animals, when she says, "Why don't you ever ask me anything personal?"

"I didn't think you wanted me to, and I don't want to make you uncomfortable. I told you before, you can share whatever you want with me—or nothing at all."

Her eyebrows slant above her eyes, and she almost looks like she's scolding me. "You shouldn't be so trusting of people. You've clearly never been burned before."

"Hah!" I can't stop the laugh that escapes. "I've been

burned plenty of times, but I've never found it all that beneficial to hold on to the hate or anger. It's never really served me except to fuck with my head. I can't control what someone else does, but I can control how I react to it. I can control how I let it affect me and impact the rest of my life. And I choose not to give those people any power over me. That said, it's a whole lot easier said than done. I'm not this Zen all the time, and it's taken a lot of work with a mental coach, but I find it's worth it. My life is happier not holding on to pain and hurt."

She stares at the ground. "I'm envious of your ability to not let your past hurt affect you, but not all of us can afford a mental coach or let our guard down so easily."

"Do you want me to ask you questions?"

"I expected you to," she says.

"That's not an answer to my question. Do you *want* me to?"

"I don't know," she whispers. "Sometimes, yes, but I'm afraid of what you'll ask. There are some things I'm not ready to answer."

I already figured as much, which is why I haven't pushed. So instead, I ask something I've already asked before. "What do you want to tell me?"

She stares at the animals as we slowly walk through the zoo, and minutes pass before she finally speaks. "I wanted to open a bakery when I was little. My mom and I used to bake together all the time, but my favorite was cookies—the kind that are ridiculously decorated. I wanted to make those for people, as well as other baked goods."

"Why didn't you?"

She side-eyes me. "Turns out I'm not that good at baking, and life got in the way," she says, her voice dipping low, and I get the sense there's a lot more about that sentence that she's not ready to tell me.

But she told me something. Something new. And my heart feels lighter knowing we're making progress and she's starting to allow herself to be vulnerable with me.

"What would you do if you didn't play football?"

"Probably something with my degrees. I double majored in math and computer science."

She stares at me, her mouth parted in a cute little O. "You really are a nerd, aren't you?"

I throw my head back and laugh hard. When I look back over at her, her smile reaches her eyes and they shimmer in the late-fall sun. "I told you I was."

"I guess I didn't really believe you. You're too ho—" Her smile disappears as her eyes widen, and she clears her throat. "You're too much of a jock."

Was she about to call me hot?

Maybe my feelings aren't as one-sided as I thought.

# THIRTEEN

# Danae

I've never been a big fan of football, or any sport for that matter. I tried soccer once when I was ten and hated every second of it. After my one and only practice, I told my mom she'd need to knock me out with a soccer ball to get me to ever play again. She laughed until she realized I was serious.

Even though I know nothing about football, when Gabe asked me if I wanted to come to one of his home games and watch him play, I couldn't say no. There was a vulnerability in his gaze when he asked that tugged at my heart. It seemed important to him that I be there, and maybe more importantly, a part of me wanted to go and support him.

Which is how I ended up here, standing awkwardly outside a VIP box, staring at a group of women all sporting large diamond rings on their fingers and wearing jerseys with their respective partner's name on them. A brunette who looks a bit like Kate Middleton wears a jersey with Fuller on the back of it. A quick glance at the "cheat sheet" Gabe made for me tells me her husband is Jack Fuller, the quarterback. Another woman with gorgeous black hair and curves that I'd kill for sits next to her. Her jersey reads

Edmonson. Another glance at the cheat sheet tells me Will Edmonson is a wide receiver. A blonde with shoulder-length hair and bright-blue eyes smiles softly at something a stunning and curvy redhead says to her. The blonde's jersey reads Fischer, while the redhead's says Carter. Matt Fischer is a tight end and Luke Carter is a fullback. Honestly, their positions are meaningless to me since I know nothing about football, but apparently they're all on the offense, at least according to Gabe's notes.

I grip the cheat sheet in my hand and nibble my lip, wondering how to approach this situation. Catered food and beverages sit on two tables at the back of the room, and there's an open chair next to Fuller's wife, but that might be presumptuous. When Gabe asked me to come to his game, I assumed I'd be sitting in the stands surrounded by hundreds of strangers. I had no idea he'd put me in a confined space with a small group of women.

They're going to want to get to know more about me—that's always the case in small groups, and it's why I've avoided being in situations like this for the past several years.

Fuller's wife stands up from her seat and moves toward one of the tables in the back, grabbing a water. When she turns around, she catches sight of me standing in the doorway, and her eyes flash with surprise before she breaks out into a radiant smile.

"Hey! You must be Danae. Come on in. We don't bite." She gestures for me to join her, and I straighten my spine and give her a small smile as I move fully into the room. At this point the other women have all turned around and offer me nothing but kind smiles.

There are no obvious signs of judgment, no questioning

looks, none of the aloofness I would expect from women married to pro footballers.

Fuller's wife holds her hand out to me. "I'm Paige. Gabe told us to expect you." She points to the black-haired woman she was sitting next to. "This is Gina," then to the blonde, "Nikki," and last to the redhead, "and Emma." Now that she's facing me, I recognize her instantly as the singer from the bar that first night I met Gabe.

I raise my hand in a wave. "Hey." God, that sounded lame.

Paige must see my discomfort because she offers me another kind smile and then says, "Here, come sit by me and we'll fill you in. Gabe said you don't know much about football."

"Not a thing, if I'm honest."

"Hang out with the guys long enough, and you'll pick it all up in no time," Nikki says.

"Easy for you to say. You grew up in this world," Gina says to Nikki.

"You watched a lot of football growing up?" I ask, and then internally wince. I know better than to ask questions because they always come back around like a boomerang.

"My dad's the coach, so living and breathing football was a requirement of growing up in the Denton household."

"You're the coach's daughter and you're engaged to a player?"

Her smile is coy. "It's a long story, but yes. My dad wasn't thrilled, but it all worked out in the end as it usually does."

What I wouldn't give for her confidence that everything works out the way it's supposed to. Living with Gabe has been the first time in two years when I've felt like I could actually breathe easy without always waiting for the other shoe to drop.

And yet, even now, there are times where I'm still waiting for the other shoe to drop, or worse—for Gabe to turn into a monster like Mitch did, which isn't at all fair to him when he's been nothing but kind to me.

Next to me, Paige takes a sip of her water before bending forward to grab something from her bag. When she pulls out a sleeve of saltines, I bite back the question on my tongue that you never ask a woman. But I don't have to wait long for my guess to be confirmed.

"Morning sickness bad today?" Gina asks her.

She groans. "Try all day sickness. I swear this kid is trying to punish me for something." She turns to me. "I'm fourteen weeks pregnant, and the morning sickness has been awful."

She rubs her still relatively flat belly affectionately, even if she does look like she's not feeling one hundred percent.

"The first Wolves baby. It's so exciting," Emma says, and I can practically see the hearts in her eyes. "I can't wait to marry Luke and pop out a brood of babies."

"You just want an excuse to jump on your man."

Her smile turns mischievous. "I don't need an excuse, but yes, I'll take one. If you knew what he could do with it, you'd want it too."

Gina throws her head back laughing, then says, "I'm plenty satisfied, thank you very much."

Paige shakes her head and then says, "Alright ladies, let's not scare Danae away with talk of babies and big dicks."

Nikki just shrugs. "I'm sure Gabe's packing."

I choke on my own saliva, and Gina grabs me a water bottle to help ease my coughing fit. Nikki smiles at my reaction, and I can't deny her words have another strange effect on me—I can't stop picturing what Gabe's dick might look like. It makes me feel like a giant creep for about thirty seconds before I decide no one will ever know the dirty thoughts filtering through my mind right now.

And frankly it's such a relief to think of a man sexually that I'm not even mad about it. It's been so long since I've felt any desire at all, let alone wanted to think about a man's anatomy and how he might use it to make me feel good. Somehow I know Gabe would never leave a woman unsatisfied.

"You know who's probably packing—"

"Emma!"

She laughs freely and the others join her. This might be the most frivolous and ridiculous conversation I've ever had, and it feels amazing. The tension that's been strangling my shoulders slowly slides away. My heartbeat steadies and I relax in my seat as the game starts.

Paige starts pointing out players, including the other three guys in the Fierce Four, which Gabe told me all about. "Oh, and there's Gabe." She points down to the field, and even though we're far away, I can tell it's him. He's got a more dominating presence on the field, but there's a calmness to him that matches the version of him I've become so familiar with. I nibble my lip as I watch him stand on the sidelines, goofing off with his teammates briefly before they start talking to their coach. Even though they tower over her, they focus on her with rapt attention and respect, and that icy case around my heart thaws a little more.

The women carry the conversation throughout the game and always make sure I'm included as they explain things or discuss popular topics, but I begin to notice they never once pry into my own life or background. They never probe me for personal information, even when I ask them something about themselves. Occasionally, one of them looks at me like they want to ask, but they never do.

I never went to college because it was too expensive, but as the game carries on and I begin to bond with these new women who accept me into the fold, I start to wonder if this is what those friendships built in dorms and sororities are like.

Without a doubt in my mind, I know Gabe is behind why they never ask me a personal question—they're all too friendly to not ask unless they were told not to. He made sure I could enjoy myself without worry about someone trying to pry into my life. He gave me an afternoon to relax and connect with these vibrant and accepting women in a way that he knew would put me most at ease, and I'm suddenly eager for the game to end so I can thank him.

Although truthfully, I don't know how to thank him for all he's already done for me.

He's given me a job, a home, friendship, and something I thought I'd never feel again—hope.

By the time the game ends in another victory for the Wolves, I'm antsy to see him. I follow Paige, Gina, Nikki, and Emma to the area outside the locker room where we wait for the guys to exit. It doesn't take long for the crowds to thin, and then the guys come out, showered and dressed in suits. But none of them steal my breath the way Gabe does. His perfectly tailored navy blue suit hugs his tall figure in all the best ways, fitting his huge shoulders and bulky biceps, while also managing not to look baggy on his trim waist.

I've caught him working out in a pair of loose gym shorts and nothing else several times over the last few weeks, and each time I have to remind myself not to stare.

I've never seen a man so fit in my entire life. I might not be able to see all of his tight, tan muscles under his suit, but knowing some of what's underneath makes my stomach flutter with unfamiliar butterflies. Those butterflies seem to take flight when Gabe's dark gaze locks on mine, and his face lights up with a brilliant smile.

I wish he was unattractive, or had some giant flaw, so that I wasn't so insanely attracted to him. My judgment with guys obviously can't be trusted if my past experience is anything to go by, but damn, do I wish I could take the leap and jump right into his thick arms.

But I can't.

A woman in my position—on the run—doesn't have the luxury of giving in to whims of the heart.

Los Angeles—and Gabe—is only a stop on the map for me. I'm more aware than ever that at any moment, Mitch could track me down. Then I'll be back on the road, heading to a new destination, and LA will be only a blip in the rearview mirror.

Knowing that doesn't make the thought of leaving any easier to swallow. It's made even more difficult by the painful truth that for the first time in as long as I can remember, I don't want to run away.

I want to stay right here.

With Gabe.

He walks over to me and stops a few feet in front of me, leaving plenty of space, while the other girls rush into the arms of their significant others.

"Did you enjoy the game?" he asks me.

"I did. A lot. The girls were super helpful in explaining everything to me."

He smiles down at me, his warm brown eyes swirling

with an affection that makes me ache. "Good. I'm glad. Maybe you can come to another one in the future then?"

*In the future.*

What kind of future do I really have? Always on the run, never letting anyone close, never feeling safe or settled.

That's not the future I want.

I want the one where I can hang out with Gabe at the zoo on my day off, or go to a game and hang out with the wives of his friends. I want the one where we share small secrets over unpacked boxes or on Post-it notes that I don't have to keep hidden in a drawer.

I want to stay here.

I just don't know how.

# FOURTEEN

# Gabe

Away games can be brutal, but they're worse when you get closer to the playoffs. There's more pressure, but without the cheering from hometown fans. The hits get harder from opposing players desperate to knock us off our pedestal. The hunger for victory gets so intense, your mouth practically waters the second you step onto the field.

In the past, my mind would hyperfocus on one thing and one thing only—football, and more specifically winning games.

At tonight's away game, my gaze kept skirting to the sidelines wishing Danae was here, and wondering if maybe she was watching on the TV in the pool house. Having her at my game last week triggered a change in me I couldn't have anticipated. For the first time in my career—my life really—I'm distracted by a woman.

I thought maybe it'd gone unnoticed—maybe I was just being too hard on myself—until we're out celebrating at a local bar and Tyler grips me by the shoulder and says, "Bro, what the fuck was up with that almost miss? You never let a guy through the pocket like that."

Romel takes a drink of his rum and Coke—likely the only one he'll have because he hasn't had an irresponsible moment since he became a single dad—and nods in agreement with Ty.

I shrug his words off like they're no big deal. "Just in my head tonight. I can practically taste the division championship and finally having a giant Super Bowl ring on my finger at the end of the season."

Ty throws his hands up. "Woah, woah, woah. Don't jinx us like that, man. Take it back!"

I laugh. "Nah, man. I'm manifesting."

Both of them look at me like I grew a second head. "What? My sister Cami is into that shit. Leave me alone." I push Ty back and he pretends he's offended for all of fifteen seconds before he breaks out in a shit-eating grin.

Dom swoops in between us, wrapping an arm around each of us, a beer in both of his hands. "What's up, fellas? Anybody interested in body shots with these two lovely ladies behind me?"

He glances over his shoulder, and we all follow his gaze to see two women who are objectively gorgeous.

"Not since college, bro," Ty says. "But I suppose I could take a walk down memory lane for these beautiful women."

The brunette rubs her body on Ty, practically serving her breasts to him on a platter, and he soaks up every minute of it. His hands rest easily on her hips as he gazes appreciatively at her body against his. "Well, hello there, beautiful. What's your name?"

"Jen," she says with a flirtatious giggle.

I take a sip of my drink as I watch him seal the deal. It's his standard move and it never fails.

"Well, Jen, I've got a mosquito bite that I was hoping you could look at for me."

She scrunches up her nose. "Um, ew?"

He shakes his head, already prepared for this response. "No, see, only saliva can really help it. Want to know where it is?"

She says, "Sure," dragging out the word with uncertainty.

He leans down, putting his mouth to her ear, whispering that it's on his dick—something I wish I didn't know, but that's what he told us once—and Romel and I exchange a glance. We've seen him do this way too many times. I can't believe it works, but I guess when you're a pretty boy like Ty you can get away with saying some of the most ridiculous shit I've ever heard.

I turn to look at Dom and see him already sucking face with the blonde who came over with Jen. Funny enough, she kind of looks like his bestie, Alayna, from this angle.

I wonder if it would totally kill his boner if I told him that.

Jen pulls back enough to look Ty in the eyes, her cheeks flushed pink as she nods. He smirks and then glances up at us. "Sorry, boys, looks like I have plans for the rest of the night."

With a two-fingered salute, he exits, his arm still wrapped around the brunette who is suddenly eager to go with him.

Dom stops sucking face with the blonde and hands her a fifty-dollar bill. "Why don't you grab another round of drinks for the table while I check in with my guys and then we can get out of here." He practically growls the last word, and she takes his fifty—a little too happily—and saunters toward the bar.

Dom faces us as if he didn't just have a girl wrapped around him. "So, what are you pussies doing tonight? I've given up on trying to get Romel laid, but I'd be happy to help you find a jersey chaser, G man."

"I think I can find my own hookup, thanks." Not that I have any intention of having a hookup, but I also don't feel like having a debate with Dom about one-night stands.

He's pro anything that doesn't come with strings, complications, or feelings—emphasis on the feelings.

He shrugs. "You guys aren't any fun."

"Guilty as charged," Romel says with a smile before taking another drink from his glass. "Maybe you should try doing something fun that won't give you an STD."

He shoots Romel a look. "I always wrap it up, so that's not a problem."

"Until you let a woman give you a blowjob who has mouth herpes."

Hand to God, I wish I could take a picture of the pure mortification that washes over Dom's face. Someone didn't pay attention in sex ed.

He grabs Romel's drink out of his hand and tosses it back. "Fuck me. That was gross." Then he points his finger accusingly at him. "Don't fucking try to ruin BJs for me. There are few perfect things in this world and that's one of them."

The blonde returns with another round of drinks that I have no plan on touching. And with one more glare directed at Romel, Dom wraps his arm around her shoulder and heads out of the bar.

Romel watches him go with a thoughtful expression on his face. "Did she look like—?"

"Yup," I answer.

He nods once. "I thought so. Do you think he realizes he's in love with his best friend?"

I'm grateful I chose not to drink any more or I likely

would've spewed it all over him. "Where the fuck did you get that idea?" And again, I wonder what everyone is seeing that I apparently haven't.

His steady gaze watches me like he's waiting for me to see what he sees, but if that's the case, he's going to be waiting a long time. "Hmm...well, I guess we'll see."

"I think you'll be waiting a long time if you think he's got a thing for Alayna."

He shrugs. "Maybe. I don't know. I think I'm pretty good at reading my closest friends. It's how I figured out you've got it bad for Danae."

My dark gaze snaps to his. "Not that impressive, since I basically already told you as much a while back."

He shrugs. "You said you were interested, but you've not glanced at a single woman all night and barely acknowledged the two bombshells that Dom brought over. While you've never been a big one-night stand kind of guy, I rarely see you turn down the opportunity to appreciate the look of a beautiful woman. Which leads me to believe your feelings are deeper than you let on."

"We're just friends—not even that, really. I mean, I'm her employer." I hate the word the moment it comes out of my mouth. I don't like calling her a friend either because it doesn't feel strong enough, but to reduce everything down to employer and employee seems even worse.

"You really want to play that line with me?"

We have a brief stare-off before I cave. "Fine. I like her. I've caught feelings and think about her all the damn time and have to actively hold myself back from getting down on one knee with how great I think she is, and I know hardly anything about her past. Happy?"

A smile spreads across his face, wider than I've seen since his wife died, and his arms shoot up. "I knew it!"

I shake my head. "You suck for calling me out, ya know."

"Eff off. Someone needed to do it. You almost missed that tackle and you never miss."

"You know it's safe to swear, right? We're in a bar. Everyone's over twenty-one."

"If I let one swear word slip in front of Kay, then that's all I'll hear for weeks. It's just easier to use the replacements until she's older and I'm not so worried about her heading off to daycare shouting the f-word to all her friends."

A chuckle escapes at the image of sweet, innocent little Kaylee saying fuck to all her little toddler friends. Yeah, he's probably right. Better safe than sorry.

"Wait...is that why you never let us come over anymore?"

"Are you seriously just now figuring that out? Y'all swear like sailors. I'm not bringing that into my house."

"Damn, man. That hurts. And here I thought we were brothers."

He smiles and then we both agree to head back to the hotel and get some sleep before our early flight back to LA in the morning. It's nice to be out with him like this and see him acting more like his old self. Grief is a nasty sonofabitch, and it's hard to watch someone you care about go through it. I'd go through hell with this man, and yet I'm completely incapable of dragging him out of the personal hell his life became when his wife died.

We part ways on our floor, him going to the right, me to the left. When I get to my room, I immediately change into some sweats and then grab the remote and lie on the bed. My phone taunts me from the nightstand, and I pick it up, only to put it down again.

I want to text Danae, but I don't know if she'd want to

hear from me. It's just...I can't fucking stop thinking about her. About how she listens to my kitchen radio while she cleans and dances around, using a spatula as a microphone. About her love of romance books and the different ones I've caught her reading over the last month. About how surprised and pleased she seems when I do something small for her.

It makes me wonder if anyone has ever done something for her just because.

Ideas start swirling in my mind, and I try to convince myself that I'm doing it because I want to be a good friend, but even I know that's not true.

My restraint breaks and I grab my phone, and before I can think too hard about what I'm doing, I send her a text.

> Is it weird that I miss you?

Almost immediately, my stomach sinks. Fuck. That's not friendly or employer-y at all. I run my fingers through my hair as I wait for her response and hope I can backtrack this. I don't even have the excuse of alcohol to fall on. What the fuck was I thinking?

I wasn't. That's the problem. I never think clearly around this woman.

As the shows on the TV turn into infomercials and my phone still remains silent, I realize she's not going to text me back. For the second time tonight, my stomach sinks, but this time in defeat.

I haven't had a girlfriend since college, and she didn't consume my attention the way Danae does, so I'm beyond rusty in handling situations like this. But her lack of response is a clear indicator that my feelings are completely one-sided.

Dejection weighs me down like lead weights on my body.

But this is all on me.

She's made her wishes clear from day one—she needed a stable job and a roof over her head, nothing more. I'm the one who went and caught feelings like a fucking idiot.

Grabbing the remote, I turn off the TV and roll over, hoping the darkness in the room will entice sleep to take over my thoughts. And as slumber finally starts to pull me down, I make one last promise in the dark.

I'm going to respect her wishes and keep things firmly in the friend zone, but I'm still going to follow through with the surprise I've got planned for her.

Because even if we're only friends, she deserves to be spoiled.

# FIFTEEN

# Danae

Fear is a nasty, vengeful bitch who loves to fuck with your head. Only this time, I'm not afraid of Mitch finding me. I'm afraid of how much Gabe has gotten under my skin and made me feel things I've never felt before—not even when I thought I was madly in love with Mitch.

Unfortunately, I think my fear might've already ruined it.

When he texted me after his away game a week ago, I didn't know what to say.

*I miss you too.*

*The house feels empty without you.*

*I wish you'd hold me when you come home.*

*I wish I could let you see all the parts of me that I hide away in the dark of my soul.*

*You deserve someone who's not such a mess and doesn't have a psycho ex after her.*

I couldn't say any of those things, even if they were all true, so instead I said nothing. And Gabe has been respectfully polite ever since he returned home.

I hate it, but I also know I'm in this situation of my own making. Now I'm forced to ask myself if I want to fix it or if it would be best to leave things as they are. If I was being fair to Gabe, I would leave things as they are. It's for the best that we maintain a distance from each other. Polite, courteous, but not friends. Bringing him fully into my life will only be messy and complicated, and he deserves so much more than that. He's too nice of a guy to be stuck with a mess like me.

But I also don't know how much longer I can take this before I break. All week long he's sent me out on errands that kept me out of the house all day while he's there, as if he doesn't want me around. I should be happy about that, about him not getting attached because I can't afford to put down roots right now, but I'm not happy about it at all. I want him to walk through the house and chat with me, or fold laundry with me because he says it makes him feel weird knowing I might be folding his underwear, or all the other small ways he interacts with me throughout the day.

All the ways he looks at me too. Like I'm precious, and I matter. He still looked at me like that this week, but the distance was more pronounced than ever before.

I can't tell him how I feel, but maybe the surprise I'm working on will show him what he means to me and how thankful I am for him. When I was walking by the room where Gabe's comics still sit in boxes, a thought struck me, and I reached out to a local shop about how to protect them and maybe display them a little better. That conversation led to a fall down the rabbit hole of grading and certification, especially once I took a box to the shop and the owner saw some rare editions that I knew nothing about. Unfortunately, the process through the company he recommended takes about ten days, so I'm still waiting. I don't know if it'll help get us back to where we were before his text, but I hope it'll move us away from whatever we've become this week.

I can admit, even if only to myself, that I want his lingering gaze and the way he made me feel like an attractive woman and not just a friend.

As I pull up to the house, my thoughts run wild with different ideas, some more outrageous than the last, that might help me get back the Gabe I've grown so attached to if my comic book plan doesn't work. My feet halt when I walk in the door to find the man who's taken over my thoughts standing there waiting for me.

Oh my God, he's going to fire me. That's what this has been about, hasn't it? The distance, the keeping me out of the house. Just as quickly as horror fills me, it's eviscerated by a sharp blade of rage. How dare he fire me just because I didn't text him back. If he knew the way I've agonized over that damn text, he wouldn't be so dismissive.

Although...wait.

He doesn't look dismissive at all.

Honestly, he looks sexy as hell in a pair of fitted jeans and a T-shirt that hugs his shoulders and biceps. His eyes peruse my body, and there's a warmth in them that makes my heart beat faster behind my ribs. With a blink, it vanishes, replaced by that polite kindness he's tossed my way this past week, and an ache develops in my belly from how badly I feel the need to get us back to where we were.

"I hope you didn't mind all the errands I had you run this week. I needed you out of the house for a surprise I was working on."

"A surprise?" Are we really that in sync that we each planned a surprise for the other? Now I really wish the comics were ready.

He tilts his head toward the hallway to the right of the kitchen that leads to a bunch of empty rooms and his gym. "Follow me," he says and then starts heading down the hall, his sock-covered feet not making a sound.

I follow, mesmerized, until he stops in front of a door that's about halfway down the hall. This is one of the larger empty rooms on this side of the house, and his gym is only two doors down on the opposite side of the hallway.

He gestures to the door. "Open it." His voice has a slight waver like he's unsure about what's on the other side. Or, maybe more accurately, my reaction to what's on the other side.

Curiosity nips at my heels and pushes me forward, but nothing could prepare me for what I find on the other side.

"What in the *Beauty and the Beast* did you do?"

My wide-eyed gaze scours the room before me that's been completely transformed into the library of my dreams. There are wall-to-wall built-in bookshelves, a wide window seat with large fluffy pillows that overlooks the backyard and the pool, and a gorgeous fireplace with an oversized chair in front of it that begs to be curled up in.

I move toward the bookshelves and scan the titles, eagerly seeing what he's selected. My fingers still as my heart gallops. The shelves are filled with romance novels—bestsellers and the most popular books as well as a variety of contemporary, paranormal, and historical. I fight back a giggle when I see the cover for a popular book about big blue aliens which I've been wanting to read.

"How...how on earth did you know I'd want these books?" It's literally hand-curated for me.

I finally turn to look at Gabe, who's still standing awkwardly at the door, his eyes locked on me and his hand crossed over his chest and gripping his shoulder. He looks anxious and worried.

"Do you like it?" he asks, and I want to scream at him for even asking.

"*Like* it? No." His face falls, and I hasten the rest of my response. "Gabe, I *love* it. You did all this for me?" I press my hand over my heart because it feels like it's going to beat right out of my chest.

No one has ever done anything like this for me. This is by far the most extreme, thoughtful, and perfect gift I could've ever received.

His shoulders sag with relief, but he's still got that embarrassed look on his face that makes my heart squeeze. "It was nothing, really. I just wanted to do something nice for you that you'd enjoy."

I'm already shaking my head before he finishes his sentence. "Don't do that, please." My voice is barely a cracked whisper as emotion swells in my throat, trapping the more important words I wish I could say. Instead I say, "This is...Gabe, this is the nicest thing anyone's ever done for me. I... Thank you."

My body moves well before my brain can catch up, and even when it does, I don't stop the forward momentum. My feet carry me across the floor until I'm standing in front of him, throwing my arms around his giant shoulders, and giving him the tightest hug I can. I don't have the words for what this means to me, but hopefully my hug will help emphasize how big a deal it is.

Except I'm not prepared for the instant zing that infiltrates my body as soon as we touch. Our chests are pressed together and his bulky arms wrap around my narrow waist, holding me close to his body. His head tilts against mine, and I can feel his breath brushing along my neck. My body thrums with awareness, and a barely contained shiver slithers through me. Everywhere we touch lights up with need until I feel like I might combust. I pull back, my arms still wrapped around his neck, and he does the same until our faces are only an inch apart. His brown eyes have darkened, and his tongue slides across his bottom lip so subtly, I might've missed it if we weren't so close. He's looking at me like I'm a juicy steak and he's a starving lion.

I didn't think this feeling was real—just something made up by romance authors with either more exciting lives than mine or better imaginations—but the joke's on me, because I've never felt more like a heroine from one of my romance novels than in this moment. My heart is beating faster than a hummingbird's, my breath is coming out in shallow pants, and there's no denying the slick between my legs from how turned on I am.

Gabe's chest heaves against mine before he swallows audibly and then closes his eyes, breaking our connection. A flash of pain streaks across his rugged features before he gently sets me down—I hadn't even noticed that he'd lifted me slightly off the ground—and releases me from his hold.

It takes effort to remove my arms from around his neck when every piece of me wants to continue holding on to him. More than that, I want him to kiss me with a desperation that scares me.

He takes a step away from me, and the cold air against my skin might as well be a bucket of ice water for the effect it has on me.

He clears his throat. "I'm glad you like it."

And then he turns tail and walks out of there like his ass is on fire, while I stand frozen in place and completely perplexed.

This incredible man just gifted me a personalized

library in his house, and then when we were on the cusp of having what would no doubt be the best kiss of my life, he bailed.

What the hell just happened?

And how do I get the kiss I'm now craving more than my next breath?

# SIXTEEN

# Gabe

"You did WHAT?"

I knew my sister would freak when I told her about Danae. I've been putting off the conversation for weeks now because I knew once I told one of them, my mom would find out and then it would become a whole big thing. But right now I'm desperate for Cami's advice, so I had to tell her the whole story.

"Can we skip past the part where you scold me for letting a stranger move in with me and move on to the part where you help me dig myself out of the giant fucking hole I've dug?"

She places a manicured finger to her forehead as she stares off at the sidewalk in front of us as we walk toward the restaurant where we're getting lunch. "Oh, little brother, I don't even know where to begin."

"Try."

She must hear the panic in my tone because she glances up at me, her eyes softening as she takes in the bags under my eyes. I slept like shit last night after spending the rest of the day avoiding Danae at all costs.

I nearly kissed the shit out of her in her library. I was an inch away and only *just* found the strength to pull away. But then I spent the rest of the day on such a hair trigger of want for her that I was convinced all it would take to push me over would be to see her standing in my house looking sexy as hell. I can't do that to her. She wants to be friends, and I swore to myself I would be okay with that.

Friends don't kiss.

But fuck, do I want to be the kind of friends who do.

"Ay *hermanito*, you've gone and done it this time."

"I know." I scrub my hands over my face. "How do I fix it? I don't want her to be skittish or uneasy with me."

She side-eyes me and her gaze turns thoughtful. "What makes you think she was bothered by your *gift*?" She emphasizes gift with a tone that suggests she thinks I went way overboard.

Obviously.

That's why I'm in this damn mess. I just wanted to do something nice for someone important to me, and now I'm not sleeping and I'm afraid to go home until I'm sure I can keep my body and desire in line. I can only imagine the horror on Danae's face if she sees me pop a boner the second I look at her.

"Gabe?"

Shit. She asked me a question. "She didn't text me when I told her I missed her."

"But that was before you built her a library?"

"Yeah."

She stares at me like I should see where she's going with this, but I have no idea. She smirks. "Okay, so how did she respond to the library?"

"She loved it. She—" I'll never forget the way her face lit up and transformed when she saw all her books. I thought she was beautiful before, but in that moment, all the shadows that hide behind her eyes disappeared and she was absolutely stunning. "She gave me a hug."

My pants suddenly feel tighter as I think about the hug I likely would've had dreams about if I'd been able to sleep. As it was, I rubbed one out thinking about what would've happened in my dreamworld if I'd completely lost my head and kissed her. But I can't go down that train of thought while I'm standing next to my sister.

And...boner gone.

"What kind of hug?" Cami asks.

I stare at her like she just asked me one of those obscure *Jeopardy!* Questions. "What do you mean what kind of a hug? It was a hug. A hug is a hug."

She's already shaking her head. "Nope. A hug is not just a hug, especially for a woman. There's the side hug when we don't want you to get the wrong idea, there's the top hug where we hug facing you, but really only barely touch upper chests and loosely wrap our arms around you before separating. Then there's the full body hug—the hug where you're holding on and touching everywhere possible, full upper bodies plastered to each other and close enough you could bury your head in her neck, your arms wrapped around her waist and her arms squeezing your neck, and neither of you want to let go." She's staring off in the distance as she describes the full body hug and then fans her face and wiggles her body like she's shaking off whatever daze she was just in before turning to me, serious as can be. "So which hug was it?"

"The last one. It was definitely the last one," I say, my voice strained as I think about the moment when Danae pulled back slightly and she looked so happy and sexy that all I wanted was to exist in her orbit for the rest of my life.

Cami stops walking, and I slow down to look back at her. "What?" I ask.

"Are you kidding me right now?"

"No..." I say, confused about the look of pure frustration on her face.

"You had a full body hug with this woman you say you're interested in and you didn't seal the deal?"

"I feel like there's a right and wrong answer to that question."

She smacks my arm. "*Órale, pendejo,*" she says with a roll of her eyes like I'm the biggest idiot known to man. "Of course there is! Did she linger while you held her?"

*Yes.*

My face must give me away because she groans in frustration and then wraps both hands around my bicep and shakes me.

"You had her in your arms and you didn't kiss her?!"

"I didn't think she wanted to be kissed!" A big part of me was convinced I was imagining the heat in her eyes, the way they dilated when she looked at my mouth. I immediately broke the hug because I was afraid I was forcing myself on her. Or worse, that she thought I built her the library in exchange for something with her. I didn't do it thinking I'd get anything from her. I did it because I wanted to. Because it felt good to make her happy.

Because I'd do anything just to see her smile.

Man, if the guys saw me now I'd never hear the end of how whipped I am—all for a woman who's not even mine.

Cami shakes her head at me. "I am so disappointed in you."

"How the hell was I supposed to know?"

She arches an eyebrow. "Answer me. Did she linger in the hug?"

She already knows the answer, but I say it aloud anyway. "Yeah."

"And when you pulled apart, was there a *moment*?"

"What do you mean?"

She rolls her eyes again like I'm being purposefully obtuse when I'm just trying to understand where I've gone wrong. "Did she look at your mouth?"

"Yeah." I don't even hesitate as my mind flashes back to her face, just inches from mine.

"*Dios mío*, you seriously don't get it, do you? She was into you! Women don't breathe this close to a man"—she holds her hand only inches from her face—"unless we want him to kiss us. She was giving you all the green lights, and what did you do? You ran out of there like the devil was on your heels."

My brows furrow as I stare at her, trying to make sense of all of this. "You're sure about this?"

"Yes."

"But you weren't even there. What if she did all that stuff, but—"

"But what? She held your body close to hers and let you breathe in front of her face just for fun? That's not how women work. If we're not interested, we keep some distance, we break out of hugs quickly so we don't give you the wrong idea. Trust me. Women are skilled in how to keep a man at a distance when we're not interested because we're so used to men not taking the hint. And even when we've been clear, men still try to push the envelope. In this case, she gave you all the go signals and you didn't take the bait."

"I didn't want to be a creep!" I vent, my frustration seeping out of me. I was trying to be a goddamn gentleman.

Cami's eyes soften. "Gabe, no one would ever confuse you for a creep. You're genuinely one of the nicest guys in the world, even if you're absolutely terrifying on the football field." As if her words have sparked an idea, she lights up. "You never doubt yourself on the field, so why are you doubting yourself so much now?"

Because it feels like I have more to lose this time—which is saying something since I've dedicated all my time and energy for most of my life into my sport.

"Danae is different than other girls I've dated. I didn't want her to...I don't know. I guess I didn't want her to feel like she was expected to be physical with me because of what I've done for her. Because that's not how it is. That's not what I want."

"What do you want?" Cami's gaze is curious, but not judgmental.

"From the very beginning, there was something that drew me to her. I think that's why I hired her." I *know* that's why I hired her.

But why did she stay?

Is she just there because she needs the money? She's made $12,000 since she started working for me, which is probably more than she would have made in several months at that bar she worked at when we met. Is it possible there's another reason she hasn't left yet?

Is it possible she stayed for me?

I've never been a man to accept life just happening to me. That's one thing Cami was definitely right about—I never doubt myself on the field. So maybe it's time to stop doubting what I feel for Danae and finally make a move.

When I get home, I go in search of her, eager to clear the air and with my sister's voice booming loudly in my head. A tour around the first floor proves fruitless, so I run up the stairs two at a time and pop my head into each open room in search of her. I peek into the room where I've left my comic books and am about to move on since I see she's not there, but my body freezes and my gaze snaps back to the boxes on the floor.

I may not have organized them the way they deserve to be on a bookshelf, but I know how many boxes I had. My heart starts pounding as I step fully into the room and count each box, looking around for the two that are missing. Dropping to my knees, I open the remaining boxes of comic books, and my stomach sinks when I realize which ones are missing—the most expensive ones, although they are all priceless to me.

She wouldn't.

My throat tightens, making it hard to swallow down the bile that threatens to come up as every warning the guys gave me starts overpowering any of my sister's encouragement from today.

I can't believe she'd do this to me. That the guys were right.

What the fuck?

A sound breaks through my freak-out, and I stand up and turn around to find Danae standing at the open door, her eyes wide.

"Did you seriously steal from me?"

# SEVENTEEN

# Danae

I try not to let the hurt of his words pierce through the wall I've built around myself over the past few years, but the downside of letting down your guard with someone is that it gives them the power to cause you pain.

And the way his accusation slices across my skin causes me a pain I'd forgotten existed.

It's been a long time since I cared about what other people thought of me. You can't afford to care about other people's opinions—negative or positive—when you're trying to survive. But I've started to care about Gabe's opinion of me. I've learned to crave the way his eyes linger on me, the smooth huskiness of his voice when he talks to me, his scent as it wraps around me whenever he's near, making me feel safe. I've found myself taking more time to do my hair or look more put together when I knew he'd be home while I was working. I've spent more time than necessary thinking of what to write on the sticky notes I leave for him, always wondering what he'd think of one response over another. I've taken care in the tasks he's given me, wanting him to be happy with how I've added to his life and made things easier for him—or at least hoped I did.

Not once did I ever expect him to look at me with so much hurt and disdain coating his handsome features, or for his voice to take on an accusing tone with a hint of anger. He stands tall, but his shoulders are slumped more than I've seen them, and while his mouth is held in a hard line, his eyes are filled with pleading, like he's desperate for me to prove him wrong.

It takes me a minute, but I finally find my voice. "No, I didn't steal from you." My own tone is more caustic than I intend for it to be, but I can feel all my fight-or-flight instincts rearing their ugly heads, and lashing out is some-times one of them—even if running is easier and safer. The fact I'm lashing out at all only accentuates how much Gabe's made me trust him and feel safe with him, which then only serves to make the pain of his accusation lance deeper.

His posture eases and he gestures to where the missing boxes used to be. "Then where are my comics?"

"I'll show you."

I gesture for him to follow me, but don't wait to see if he actually does. My body is strung tight, my pulse racing, anger and hurt swirling through me like a vicious tempest raging in the middle of the sea. When I reach the doors to my library—no, not mine, not after his reaction—*the* library, I step aside and gesture to the opposite side of the room where he'd left several bookshelves bare for me to fill with whichever books I wanted.

Instead, I'd filled them with his collector's and special edition comics, all now covered in protective sleeves with the certification and grading paperwork in the back. I don't say a word as he walks over and removes one from the shelf, noticing the paperwork, which he pulls out carefully. He reads it over silently and then his shoulders relax as if a huge weight has been removed.

If only I felt such relief instead of the bitter hurt that is slowly suffocating me.

He spins around and his eyes hold both an apology and appreciation. I'm not sure I'm interested in either at the moment. Right now, whatever excitement I felt about this gift for him has been wiped away, and I want nothing more than to be alone in the pool house until I can resurrect the walls I never should've let down around him. This wasn't how today was supposed to go at all, and now it feels like my gesture is tainted, even if I can see the gratefulness in his gaze.

"You got these certified?"

"Yeah."

He glances back at the shelf and then back to me. "When did you do this?"

"A week and a half ago."

His features slacken with surprise. "A week and a..." It's fascinating watching his reaction. I can practically see his brain putting everything together and also realizing how horrible his accusation was, but my armor is already wrapping around me, keeping me safe from his judgment or his worthless apologies. If he honestly thinks I would steal from him after the past six weeks, then he clearly doesn't think very highly of me. And why should he? I'm just the help.

Emotion swells in my throat, but I swallow it down and blink away the stinging in my eyes. No fucking way am I crying in front of him.

"They're all there. You can double-check," I say, my

tone neutral, but my expression no doubt lacking any warmth or friendliness.

He drops his head, staring at the comic in his hand and then back at me. "I shouldn't have jumped to that conclusion. I don't know why I did."

I shrug like it doesn't bother me. "It's okay." It's not.

He swallows, his Adam's apple bobbing thickly in his throat, and I hate that a part of me still wants to move closer to him, to inhale his scent and feel his big, sturdy arms wrapping around me again.

Instead, I spin on my toes and move to exit.

"Danae," he shouts. I stop, but I don't turn around.

"I'm sorry."

"I said it's okay."

"But it's not," he says, and I can sense him moving closer. "It's not okay at all. I'm so sorry. I—"

"Don't worry about it, Gabe. I need to get back to work."

I don't bother waiting for him to say something else. I doubt it would matter anyway. Words are useless. Then again, maybe that's why I'm having such a hard time with his accusation, because his actions have always implied he trusted me, even when he had no reason to.

I get back to the pool house and lean my back against the door, tipping my head back and closing my eyes. I ignore the stray tear that leaks out, but I can't ignore the piercing pain in my chest.

One more week. I'll stay for one more week and then I need to move on. I've already been in LA longer than the last few places, and I've made enough to get started somewhere else. I should move on, move away from Gabe and all the feelings he stirs up in me.

The pain sharpens at the mere thought of starting over

again. I'm so tired of always starting over, of never feeling settled.

*You felt settled here,* a voice whispers in my head.

I did, and Gabe had to go and ruin it.

# EIGHTEEN

# Gabe

I've done some seriously stupid shit in my life, but nothing as stupid as accusing the woman I'm falling in love with of stealing from me. It's been two days since that horrible lapse of judgment and Danae has avoided me at every turn. She's not even responding to my sticky notes or leaving me any of her own.

I've looked.

I know she's been in the house because everything is immaculately clean, but every time I've tried to see her, she's nowhere to be found. When I called Cami and told her what happened, she called me an idiot and hung up on me. I probably deserved that.

Which leaves me only one other option for getting female advice from someone who's messed up before and knows what it takes to fix things.

"You got a minute, Coach?" I ask as I knock on the door frame of the conference room that Coach Fairbright tends to use as her makeshift office.

She glances up from the tablet in her hands. "Sure, Romero. What's up?"

I walk in and close the door because I don't need the other coaching staff walking by and overhearing this. Or the other players for that matter. When I sit down in the chair across from her desk, she sets the tablet down and arches a brow. "You're not about to tell me you're retiring, are you?"

"No. No, I'm definitely not retiring, at least not anytime soon and barring any serious injuries."

Her shoulders relax. "Thank God. I did not want to have to replace you when we're on a winning streak."

"Nah, it's nothing like that. It's, uh, actually not football related at all."

She tilts her head to the side and her eyes seem to sparkle with amusement. "Color me intrigued. What's up?"

"How'd you fix things with Daniel?"

Her brother, Mark, was a firefighter and died about six months ago. She'd been dating his best friend and fellow firefighter, Daniel, at the time and we were all waiting for the announcement that she was engaged. We were not expecting her to take a week off while she grieved the sudden death of her brother only to return to work announcing that she'd dumped her boyfriend of over a year. She became hyperfocused on work, and in some respects, it paid off—our team is performing better than ever under her guidance—but in others, it left us all to worry if she was okay. It was hard watching her deal with her grief, but we were all relieved when she and Daniel got back together. She's so much happier now, and I'm hoping she'll have good advice for how to fix things between Danae and me.

She sits back in her chair and crosses her arms. "That is definitely not football related. I'm going to need a little more information from you before I go spilling all my mistakes to one of my players."

"There's a woman...I hired her to be my housekeeper

because I inadvertently got her fired from her job as a waitress and I just felt like she really needed a break. It was one of those *what would I want someone to do if this was my sister* moments, but I was also crazy drawn to her, and then I started leaving her sticky notes because I didn't want to intimidate her, and I built her a library in one of the empty rooms in my house because I wanted to do something nice for her. Then we had a moment, and my sister Cami thinks I'm an idiot because Danae was giving me all the go signals and I totally fumbled the situation by bailing because I was afraid I was pushing her. Then I accused her of stealing from me, and now she's not talking to me, and I haven't seen in her in two days, but I know she's around because my house has never been cleaner, and I don't know how to fix it."

I heave out a breath and finally look up at my coach to see her eyes wide and her mouth parted. "Holy shit, I've never seen anyone word vomit like that before."

I bury my head in my hands. "I fucked it all up and I need help."

"Uh, yeah. I can see that." She rubs a finger over her eyebrow and then leans her elbows on the desk. "There's a lot to unravel from what you just spewed out, but what I gather is that there's a woman you're interested in, who works for you as your housekeeper, and you accused her of stealing from you. Is that correct?"

"That's the gist, yeah."

"Okay, and you came to me for help..."

"Well, yeah. I figured since you have recent experience with having to fix a relationship, you might be my best bet."

"Ah..." she says with a nod of her head. "Here's the thing, Gabe. I never accused Daniel of anything, so it's a bit different. I hurt Daniel, yes, and that's something I'm always going to be sorry for, but when you accuse someone of something, especially if they didn't do it, that breaks down the trust you've established. It causes doubts to form where there weren't any before. Do you have reason to believe she might have had feelings for you too?"

I can't ignore that she uses the past tense, but I swallow down my emotions and reply, "I think so, or at least my sister thought so based on an interaction we had when I built her a library in my house. She likes to read," I tack on, which is probably unnecessary but it seems important to me.

"You built her a library? I know you said that when everything else spilled out of your mouth, but somehow it didn't quite register until now." The shock on Coach Fairbright's face is almost laughable. She isn't much older than I am, although I've never outright asked her age. "You do realize that's like every book lover's dream come true. That's also incredibly romantic when you think about it."

"I'm trying not to think about it right now because then all I can think about is how I ruined it. She did something incredibly thoughtful for me too, and instead of trusting her like I have from the beginning—even when all the guys thought I was crazy—I suddenly believed the worst of her."

"How come?"

I shrug and fall back against the chair. I've been asking myself that since it happened. Why did I doubt her when she'd never given me a reason to? "I think maybe it was my own insecurities getting the best of me."

She arches a brow. "You think?"

"Okay, fine. I know it was. I was insecure about her feelings and where we stand. But you gotta understand, Coach, I've never felt this way for a woman before. Never. She makes me feel...fuck, I don't know. I'm not good with words and my head's all tangled around this mess, but from the moment I saw her, it felt different. I wanted to protect her, to know her, to just be near her. I never wanted to hurt her."

"You need to tell her that, Gabe. I think your best bet now is to be honest. Brutally fucking honest. What do you have to lose at this point? If she's already pushing you away, then this might be your only chance for a Hail Mary."

I rub my thumb into the palm of my hand and let her advice sink in. "I'm falling for her," I murmur.

"Kinda sounds like you've already fallen," she replies, her voice soft and gentle like she knows I've been put through the emotional wringer and am barely hanging on.

"What if I messed this up for good and there's no way to fix it?"

I glance up at her and she gives me a soft smile. "Speaking from experience, there's almost always a way to fix it, but timing is everything. The longer you leave things unresolved, the worse it gets, and the harder it becomes to fix it. But if she knows you at all, Gabe, she'll know your heart is always in the right place. It's just your head and your mouth that sometimes get you in trouble."

"Yeah, I guess you're right. Although it's never gotten me into trouble quite like this."

"Just be grateful Dom wasn't involved."

I chuckle, but it's half-assed, my heart still too heavy thinking about the conversation I need to have with Danae. If I can even get her in the same room with me.

But Coach is right; at this point, I've got nothing left to lose.

# NINETEEN

# Dande

The sound of the back door opening causes me to perk up from my seat on the barstool where I've been waiting not so patiently for Gabe to come home. I've been avoiding him and wallowing in my own hurt.

But enough's enough.

I've been running away from my biggest problem for so long, I never noticed how much I'd started running away from *every* problem. The more time I've had to think about it, the more I've realized ignoring Gabe is childish and won't solve anything. Am I still hurt that he assumed the worst? Yes. But in the last month and a half, Gabe has made me feel safe, allowing me to share bits and pieces of myself with him that I haven't shared with anyone in years. If I can't be honest with him about how much his accusation hurt, then having feelings for him is pointless.

While developing feelings for Gabe was never part of the plan, I can no longer deny them. Up until the other day, he had torn down so many of my walls with his tenderness, thoughtfulness, humor, and respect that it's been impossible to resurrect them all. Hiding away and avoiding him doesn't make those feelings go away. It doesn't make the longing for his strong arms or his booming laugh go away just because I'm hurt and still a little mad. And I've had to come to terms with the knowledge that in order to move forward, I can no longer avoid him.

More importantly, I don't think I can avoid telling him the secret I've kept from him either. I want him to know my truth—a truth I haven't shared with anyone since my cousin —and understand the situation I'm in and the reason I've relied on his generosity for so long.

A knot twists painfully in my stomach as I think about what happened to my cousin for helping me. An Internet search one night confirmed what I'd already feared. Her obituary didn't say how she died, but her smiling face in the photo that accompanied it will haunt me forever. Everyone who's ever tried to help me get away from Mitch has suffered for it, but I'm so tired of being alone and keeping everyone at arm's length.

Especially Gabe.

He deserves to know the truth. I don't know what things will look like moving forward—if he'll be the one avoiding me from now on, or worse, kick me out of his house for potentially putting him in danger—but I can't keep this from him anymore.

His footsteps slap against the smooth tile of his floor as he moves closer to where I sit in the kitchen, waiting. My back is ramrod straight and my legs are crossed at the knee. I keep my shoulders back, exuding a confidence I don't really feel.

I've survived harder things than being honest with Gabe. I can get through this.

I hope.

His steps get closer, and I turn toward the entrance at

the same time that he passes the threshold. His forward progress stops immediately as his gaze locks on me. My breath freezes in my lungs for a split second, a sharp stab of pain making my stomach clench as I remember his face and tone as he accused me of stealing from him. It's only made worse by the fact that it came after he gave me the best gift of my life and we had a moment where I wanted him to kiss me so badly, I was nearly desperate for it.

"We need to talk," I say, my voice tight.

"We need to talk," he says at the same time.

For a second we're both still, and then a small smile cracks my face and the corners of his mouth twitch up, his eyes lighting like I'm so used to when he looks at me.

Wanting to soften my approach, I suggest, "Want to sit on the couch?"

He nods and follows me out to the living room. We both settle on opposite ends of the couch, and time seems to tick by painfully slowly until it feels like we've been sitting together in silence for hours, when it's barely been a minute.

"Do you want to go first?" I ask, mainly to buy myself a little time because it's hard talking about Mitch on a good day, but with things already strained between Gabe and me, it makes it even harder.

"Sure," he says as he twists his body to face me. His expression is the sincerest I've ever seen it. "I'm sorry. I know they're just words and don't mean much, but I have to say them. I was feeling insecure myself, but that was no excuse for accusing you of something I know you'd never do. I trust you, Danae. I know we're still getting to know each other, and maybe I'm too trusting, but I have no doubt you would never do something like that. Please don't avoid me anymore. I can't stand not seeing you or talking to you. I mi—"

"I'm on the run," I blurt out, my voice shaky but clear. I don't mean to interrupt him, but hearing him say that he trusts me when I've been keeping this huge secret from him that could potentially impact him too has the words coming out uncontrollably. But once they're out, a weight seems to lift off my shoulders.

Gabe's posture immediately changes from falsely relaxed to on guard, his gaze turning sharp and protective. "Do you need protection?"

And this is why I'm falling so hard for this man, even after what happened the other day. He didn't ask whom I was running from or what I did. He asked about my safety, and I can't tell him what that kind of blind faith in me means to me. That alone reassures me that what he just said was true. His accusations were more about him than me, although what he could be insecure about, I have no idea.

"I think your house is plenty secure enough since it's in a gated community. You've given me more safety than I've had in almost two years."

He frowns, like the idea of me not being safe for such a long time hurts him. "Who are you running from?"

Gabe rarely asks me personal questions, instead choosing to let me share what I want when I'm ready, so it throws me off that he asks such a direct question now.

My heart beats a little faster just thinking his name. "My ex, Mitch."

That protective look comes back into Gabe's eyes, but he doesn't say anything, so I continue. "Things were good for the first few months we were together. He was always buying me things and making me feel special, but what I didn't notice is how those things were always attached to small remarks he'd make to tear me down in subtle ways. Like buying me lingerie and telling me how good I'd look in it when I lose a couple of pounds. Or making me feel like I wasn't smart enough for college because I barely graduated from high school, even though he knew that I'd done so poorly because I'd been working since my mom and I were barely scraping by. And then when my mom died, I very nearly dropped out, and would have if it wasn't for a teacher who told me I could push through hard things." I think about that teacher often and her faith in me. Her words have soothed me during some of the hardest times in my life, especially in the last year when there were many days where I felt like it'd be better to just give up.

"I didn't have a lot of friends or family, so it was easy for him to isolate me." I look down at my hands. "I'm embarrassed it took me so long to see what he was doing. I wish I could say that I saw him for the monster he was after the first time he hit me, but I didn't. He made me think it was my fault and then was so apologetic afterward. He promised it was a onetime thing and I believed him. It wasn't."

Not even close.

"The last time—" Emotion chokes me as I think back to that day, smiling at the male store clerk and saying thank you, and then Mitch's rage when we got home. He beat me so badly there are chunks of time I can't remember at all. And then poor Mrs. Crawford. "My neighbor found me barely breathing and unconscious. She died suddenly a week later, and I wrote Mitch a note ending things and got the hell out of there."

Gabe's stormy brown eyes swirl with so many emotions, I can't read them all.

"I had been in my new town for a month, working as a waitress, when I looked out the window and saw him staring at me from inside a car. He smiled, waved, and then drove away. When I got to the place I'd been staying at, he'd left a note on my door." I'll never forget the words that looked so innocent, but carried a heavy threat behind them. *See you soon love. Don't forget who you belong to.* "I packed a bag and jumped on the first bus. I've lived my life that way ever since. He usually finds me within a couple of months, and then I have to move on to somewhere new."

"And that's how you ended up in LA?"

I nod. "I was in Boston, and LA was the first domestic flight available."

I nibble my lip and twist my fingers in my lap. "I think it's become a game for him," I murmur the fear that's been building. "I think he likes to toy with me. He likes keeping me scared, never letting me settle enough to let my guard down."

"How does he keep finding you?"

"I don't know for sure. He's got a lot of connections. His family is super wealthy so I'm sure his money is getting him access to resources most people wouldn't have. He... In Boston, he found me because I'd reconnected with my cousin. She was the only one who knew I was there. He called me from her phone and that's how I knew he'd found me."

His body stiffens. "He called you from her phone? Have you talked to her since?"

Tears fill my eyes and my nose burns from the pressure to cry. I shake my head, but can't speak. At some point I'll need to actually voice the fact that she's dead, but Gabe's smart enough to figure out what I'm not able to say out loud.

Gabe scoots closer and lays his hand palm up on the couch next to my thigh. I place my hand in his and he wraps his fingers around mine, the heat from our palms sending warmth up my arm and soothing me slowly.

"You're safe now. I'm not going to let him get to you."

"You can't make that kind of promise, Gabe."

His gaze is fierce and determined. "Watch me."

I squeeze his hand, my heart longing for him and his promises. "Every single person who's helped me has suffered for it. I can't add you to that list."

"It's too late."

My eyes shoot to his and my heart seizes at the serious expression on his face.

He continues. "You're living in my house. If he finds you, he's going to know I'm helping you. I'm in this now whether you like it or not; no sense in fighting it."

He's right. I know he's right. Hell, I knew it when I agreed to live here—wasn't it his gated community that was such a draw for me?—but hearing him say it and knowing the reality of what could happen to him makes me want to curl up in a ball and cry.

"I'm so sorry, Gabe. I should've told you the truth from the very beginning. Or better yet, I never should've come here."

He's already shaking his head before I finish. "Don't go there. I want you here, Danae. I..."

He cuts himself off, and I glance up at him, my lashes damp from the tears that have accumulated in my eyes. "You what?"

# TWENTY

# Gabe

I can't tell her that I think I'm falling for her and there's nowhere else I'd want her to be than in the safety of my house. She just admitted to me that she had an abusive ex and is on the run. What kind of man then adds to her burden by saying, "Oh hey, by the way, that sucks about the ex, but I've got feelings for you so I'm going to make your current living situation awkward." Only a jackass would do that to someone.

I won't do that to her.

A tear escapes down her face, and I gently wipe it away, brushing my thumb across the apple of her cheek. Her eyelids lower slightly and her gaze fills with tenderness and lust. It's a heady combination I quickly ignore. I may have come home with every intention of apologizing and expressing my feelings to her, but her confession has only confirmed that I need to shove my feelings firmly in a box, never to see the light of day.

So much about her makes sense now, and I will do whatever it takes to make sure she feels like she has some stability in her life—even at the expense of my feelings.

"Gabe? What were you going to say?"

I pivot, and while it's not what I originally was going to let slip, it's still true. "I'm glad you told me. Thank you for trusting me, especially when I don't really deserve it after the other day."

"I overreacted too. If the roles were reversed, I probably would've thought the same thing. It just hurt."

"I never want to hurt you, Danae. And I don't want you to think that I have doubts about you or don't trust you. I've trusted you from the beginning."

"I know you have," she says. "Thank you for making me feel safe enough to trust you with my secret. It's been a long time since I've allowed myself to get close to someone," she murmurs, her eyes still heavy-lidded and her upper body leaning closer to me. Her hand is still gripped gently in mine, and there's a pull between us that has my body leaning closer. Her breath fans my face, and it takes every ounce of strength I possess to lean away from her instead of following the direction my body wants to go.

I let go of her hand and place it delicately on the couch, while shifting my body to make it less conspicuous that I'm putting more physical distance between us. Her brows furrow and her mouth parts as if she's about to speak, but I'm saved by my phone buzzing in my pocket.

"Sorry. One sec," I say as I pull it out to see who's calling—and silently thanking the universe for this easy out. "Hey Coach, what's up?" I ask as I stand and move toward the floor-to-ceiling window that overlooks my backyard.

Coach Fairbright doesn't usually call me, especially since I only saw her a couple of hours ago, so I know it's important. "Hey Gabe, sorry to call you like this, but Miller just broke his ankle playing a pickup game with some buddies. Denton is chewing him out for going against his contract as we speak, but we need to rework the line. I'm calling an emergency meeting for the defense, so I'll need you to come in an hour early to practice tomorrow so we can go over the new strategy."

"You got it, Coach. Need me to call anyone for you and fill them in?"

"Could you call Dom, Romel, and Ty? I've already got a couple of other folks calling some of the other guys."

"Sure thing. Consider it done."

"Thanks, Gabe." The relief is clear in her voice, and I imagine she's going to spend the rest of her night going over the playbook. "Hope everything's going okay with your girl. Have a good rest of your night."

"Yeah, you too," I say, trying to maintain my composure, even as my stomach tightens at how differently today has gone than I had hoped it would when I came home.

We hang up, and I turn back to Danae as I pocket my phone. "Sorry about that."

She clears her throat, her tears now completely dried up. "No need to apologize. Everything okay?"

"Just an injured player. I gotta call the other guys and let them know."

She nibbles on her lip, looking down at her lap and then back at me. "I..." She pauses and her gaze searches mine, worry creasing her brows before a hint of disappointment passes over her features. "I just wanted to say thank you again for the library."

I swallow hard, trying—and failing—not to think about how good it felt to have her in my arms. "It's no big deal."

She pushes on her knees as she stands from the couch. "It's a very big deal to me."

She walks forward, closing the gap between us and my heart races the closer she gets, but I lock down any emotions that threaten to rise and give away how badly I want her.

"If anything, I'm the one who should be thanking you." Emotion clogs my throat as I think about how she cared for my comics in a way no one has since my dad. "Thank you for displaying my comic books and protecting them like I probably should have done years ago. I'm sorry I ruined it."

She stops beside me and tilts her head up to look at my face. "I don't think it's ruined anymore." Her gaze drops to my mouth for a millisecond before she pushes up on her tiptoes and places a kiss on my cheek. "Thank you for being you, Gabe Romero. You're one of a kind." Her voice is soft and she's so close, all the blood in my head goes straight down to my cock with how much I ache to hold her.

"I guess I should leave you to make those calls and get back to work myself." She doesn't say anything else as she moves confidently out of the room and back toward the kitchen.

I watch her go with an equal ache in my heart and cock, wishing with everything in me that our circumstances were different.

But wishing never got me anywhere when I was a kid, and it sure as shit doesn't change things now.

Over the next several days, I stick to my old schedule—the one I held religiously before Danae moved in. Practice, gym, going over game tape, hanging with the guys. Danae and I fall into a routine that feels both comfortable and fraught with tension.

I try to ignore the way her eyes linger on mine, which I'm only aware of because it's so difficult to pull my gaze away from her. She's intriguing, resilient, and beautiful inside and out. It's an intoxicating combination, and it takes every ounce of consciousness to remember that we can only be friends.

But sometimes...sometimes it feels like we're both feeling this unspoken connection between us, the same one I felt almost two months ago at the bar when I first laid eyes on her.

Our Post-it notes continue going back and forth, but I find myself second-guessing everything I write, afraid that it might reveal too much about how I really feel. Knowing I'll be leaving tomorrow for an away game versus Arizona eases some of the strain I feel every time I'm home. I just have to get through tonight, and then I'll get a two-day reprieve from the only woman who's ever made me feel both weak and strong at the same time.

But tonight proves to be a greater temptation than I'm prepared for. When I get home, I find Danae in the kitchen in a pair of black booty shorts that hug her luscious ass and a tight white tank top with five buttons that go from between her breasts to midway down her stomach. The first three are undone, showing off a drool-worthy amount of cleavage.

*Fuck me.*

She looks up from what she's stirring on the stove and smiles at me, and that smile does me in more than her sexy outfit. God, she's so fucking beautiful when she's happy.

"Hey, you're home just in time. I made homemade pasta sauce and it's almost ready. I'm making spaghetti and meatballs. Hungry?"

"Starved," I say, my voice tight, but nowhere near as tight as my pants have suddenly become.

"Great. Want to wash up? It should be ready as soon as you're done."

"Sure," I choke out and then make a hasty retreat to the downstairs bathroom. When I close the door, I lean on the sink and stare at my expression in the mirror. "You can do this," I whisper to myself. "Pull your shit together, Gabe. You can and will resist this woman."

I splash some water on my face and then wash my hands, all the while repeating the words in my head and hoping they give me the strength to get through dinner with her.

When I reenter the kitchen, she's already moved to the attached dining room and set the table. I stop in my tracks when I see candles on the table. She glances up at me and must see the curiosity in my gaze. Shrugging her shoulder, she shoots me that sexy-as-sin smile again and says, "I hope you don't mind. I find candles really calming, and I know you leave tomorrow for your away game, so I figured you could use a nice, relaxing night at home."

I swallow thickly. "I don't mind."

Except candles make me think romance, and romance makes me think of pushing all the dishes off the table and eating Danae for dinner instead.

My cock gets painfully hard in my pants, and I quickly take a seat, hoping she didn't notice the large bulge.

Instead of sitting across from me like she used to, she sits next to me. It's both a testament to how far we've come and how safe she feels here, and absolute fucking torture. I can smell her unique scent—a combination of her shampoo and the hand lotion she wears—and see the way her eyes crinkle when she smiles at me. My fingers ache to slide through her hair and pull her mouth to mine, so instead, I pick up my fork and dig in.

The first bite explodes on my tongue with rich tomato

flavors, and I close my eyes in bliss and let out a moan. "Shit, this is good."

"Thanks. I used to love cooking, but never really had the time to play around with recipes."

"Well, feel free to take as much time as you want cooking. I'll sample it all. This is delicious."

Her smile turns pleased and she takes her own bite, nodding like she agrees with my assessment.

"Don't tell my mom I said this, but this might be the best spaghetti I've ever eaten."

She laughs. "Would your mom take offense?"

"Eh,"—I shrug—"probably not. But she has a reputation for being the best cook in our family, and we have a big family. She's gotten used to getting all the compliments."

"Does your family live nearby?"

"My sister, Camila—or Cami, as most people call her— does. My mom and little sister, Ella, live in San Diego. I also have a bunch of aunts and uncles that live down there. I try to get down to visit more often during the offseason, but it's hard during the season."

"I bet. You've been very busy. I've hardly seen you this week."

By design, but I don't tell her that. "Yeah, we've had to make some adjustments so I've been watching a lot of game tape when I'm not at practice."

She looks down at her plate, her fork pushing her spaghetti around. "That makes sense."

Something about how she says it puts me on edge. "What is it?"

She looks up at me, a guilty expression in her eyes and her mouth twisted to the side like she's chewing on the inside of her cheek. I hate how unsure she looks. "I wasn't sure if maybe you were avoiding me after our heavy conversation."

Shit. Apparently I haven't been as subtle as I thought. Worst of all, I can tell she's thinking all the wrong things about why I've been avoiding her. But I can't actually tell her why I haven't been around much because that would mean laying my feelings out on the table and potentially making shit even more awkward.

"No. Just bad timing with where we're at in the season and having to make adjustments due to other players getting injured. That's all."

She nods, but I don't think she fully believes me. Her gaze is cautious as she watches me, and the rest of our conversation feels stilted compared to the easy flow we usually have.

When we go our separate ways at the end of the night, I vow to be better when I get back from Arizona.

I don't know how, but I doubt it will be any harder than the dance we're already doing.

# TWENTY-ONE

# Dande

The clamor and clang of Gabe working out in his home gym alerts me to his location. I move swiftly in that direction, mentally preparing myself for the confrontation I know we need to have. He's been careful with me since I told him about Mitch in a way that makes me fume with frustration.

I'm not some delicate flower that will break easily. If what Mitch has put me through didn't break me, then I'm not sure anything can.

I see the way Gabe watches me, especially when he thinks I'm not looking. I know what it looks like when a man is attracted to me, and Gabe's clearly fighting that attraction with everything in his soul. What I can't figure out is why. I thought I made it obvious the other night with our romantic dinner, but then he left for Arizona the next day and when he got back he was treating me like one of the guys which was both awkward and confusing—for both of us.

I'm done letting Gabe hide from me. I need to confront my feelings for him as much as he needs to admit his feelings for me. Surprisingly, that idea doesn't make me panic with fear.

It's been a long time since I've wanted a man to touch me or kiss me, but I know Gabe's touch would never be painful. He might be huge, but he'd never use his body to dominate me in a way that made me afraid. He's far too considerate.

When I get closer to his gym, I slow my steps. Even mentally preparing myself for what I'll likely see doesn't come close to diminishing the effect of seeing Gabe exercising. He always works out in just a pair of loose basketball shorts that hang off his hips. When I stop right outside the door, he's on his back lifting up a bar that's got to be holding over two hundred pounds, but he pushes it up as if it weighs nothing. His muscles ripple under his smooth light-brown skin, the tattoos on his arms and shoulders on display. He grunts as he holds the bar up before slowly lowering it down, and the sound sends an instant zing through my body. He does a few more reps and then places the bar back on its rack. When he stands, a few sweat beads slide down his toned stomach and my mouth waters. The silver cross he always wears hangs between his pecs, and his V cut draws my eyes south. A thin strip of dark hair leads from his belly button down into his shorts, and I watch as a line of sweat rolls down his torso in the same direction my eyes went.

Sweat should not be sexy, but on Gabe it is.

His body is a giant, bulky work of art that should terrify me given my history, but instead, I've never felt safer than I do when he's near.

I want those arms wrapped around my body. I want his lips on mine. I want to taste the salt of his skin and feel his muscles ripple under my fingers.

I want him, and I'm done fighting it. Whether he knows it or not, so is he. We're not going to keep doing this dance around each other anymore.

He moves effortlessly across his gym and then stops in front of the mirrored wall and the free weights. I can't see which weight he grabs from here, but given its size, I'm assuming it's heavy. Yet he curls it up to his bicep with ease. My panties get damp as I rub my thighs together in a lame attempt to ease the ache building in my core. My peaked nipples scrape against my V-neck shirt.

Gabe brings out something in me I'd long forgotten—pure, unadulterated arousal.

I step just inside the door, and his gaze shoots to me in the mirror. His eyes instantly heat with desire, but in a blink, he's carefully composed his expression.

Nope. No more of that.

My steps are smooth and unhindered as I walk to stand directly behind him. He turns around and we stand toe to toe. His chest rises and falls with rapid pants that could be excused from his workout if I hadn't already seen how controlled his breathing was before I entered the room. He can't school his expression as well when I'm this close to him, and my own breath gets trapped in my lungs when I'm faced with the full force of his lust.

I don't even attempt to hide my own, or the way my gaze slides down his body followed by my hand. He shudders the second I touch his naked chest and then grips my wrist, stopping its descent.

"What are you doing?" His voice is gravelly.

"What does it look like I'm doing?"

He swallows thickly, his brown eyes darkening. "W-we shouldn't."

"Why not?" I whisper, moving closer and allowing my body to graze his, my gaze bouncing between his lips and his eyes.

He pauses like he's considering his response. "You work for me."

"Boss and employee romances are hot," I say with a sassy grin. He's not going to deter me on this. He's the first selfish thing I've let myself want in a long time, and I'm not leaving this room until I've kissed him at the bare minimum.

He shakes his head as if that answer isn't good enough. I can't tell if this honestly bothers him or if it's just the most convenient excuse he can come up with.

He closes his eyes, breaking our connection. "You don't owe me anything," he chokes out.

I tilt my head. This man continues to surprise me in all the best ways. "Gabe, look at me," I whisper.

His eyes pop open, heated and tortured. I keep my hand on his hot skin, feeling his heart pound furiously in his chest.

"I'm not standing here because I feel like I owe you something. I am grateful for the opportunity you gave me, but more than that, I'm standing here because I want you, more than I've let myself want anything or anyone for a very long time. You make me feel safe and cared for. You're kind, generous, funny, and humble—even when by all accounts you shouldn't be. I don't want to fight this pull to you anymore, and I hope you don't either."

"You're fired," he says, a split second before his lips crash on mine and suck all the breath from my body.

Gabe's kiss is a debilitating mix of tender and passionate at the same time. My knees weaken, and he wraps an arm around my waist, holding me tight to his body as his tongue licks across the seam of my lips. I grant him access without a second thought and moan as his tongue glides seductively against mine, licking into my mouth in ways that I imagine mimic how he might lick me much, much lower. Just thinking about it makes my clit throb, and my body rubs against his. His hard cock is like a thick, steel rod between us that I desperately want to feel inside me.

He breaks the kiss, but only so his mouth can move down over my jaw and then my neck, sucking on a spot that feels like it's connected directly to my clit.

"Don't stop," I plead.

He doesn't respond apart from a groan and then kisses down my chest. He moves my shirt up and grips one breast over my bra while he pulls the other cup down and sucks on my hard nipple. I hold his head to my breast as I watch his every movement with heavy-lidded eyes.

He moves his hands to hold my hips as he lowers himself all the way to his knees, and I feel like I've died and gone to heaven. He looks up at me, and our gazes lock as he grabs the top of my yoga pants and pulls down, dropping a kiss to my navel and then lower as he takes my thong with my pants. He tugs them off my legs completely and throws them somewhere behind him, but neither of us bother to look away from each other, not even when he dips down and licks up the seam of my pussy.

My legs shake, and his eyes finally close with a look of pure bliss on his face as he groans, throws one of my legs over his shoulder, and then buries his head between my legs. I cry out as pleasure hits me full force, and I'm grateful Gabe has such huge hands that he can hold my body up as he ravishes my pussy like it's the best fucking meal of his life. Without that grip on me, I'm convinced my legs would give out.

"Gabe, I'm so close," I whimper, gripping the strands of his hair and holding his head against me.

He growls, and the sound vibrates against my clit in such a way that stars start to cloud my vision.

"Fuck," I cry out as he slips a finger inside and curls it against a spot that intensifies whatever the hell he's doing on my clit. My orgasm hits me like a two-ton truck, and I scream his name as my body shakes from the unrelenting release.

Before it's even subsided all the way, he picks me up and carries me to the sturdy wooden table where he stores extra towels and water bottles. Holding me with one hand, he uses the other to grip the side of the long table and flip it up so everything slides off it and onto the floor. Then he sets it down and lays me back, curling his body over mine so he can take my lips in another heated kiss. I've never tasted myself in a kiss before, and there's something so naughty about it, but it also makes me feel completely uninhibited and connected to him. I grip his face, holding his head to mine so I can slide my tongue into his mouth and kiss him harder. He groans and his body weight on top of me grows heavy, but not suffocating.

His hard cock is still covered by his shorts, but is rubbing that spot between my legs that's still sensitive from my barely faded orgasm.

My mind is foggy with a post-orgasm haze, but I'm not so far gone that I don't notice when he stiffens and drops his head to my chest with a murmured, "Fuck."

"What's wrong?"

"I don't have any condoms."

That makes sense. I can't see him having a ton of sex in here. He's pretty religious about his workouts. I run my fingers over his hair. "That's okay. We can go up to your room."

He lifts his head to look at me. "I don't have any condoms at all."

My brows furrow ever so slightly. There's no way this

guy was celibate before we met. He's hot, rich, and famous. I've seen the way women look at him. "You forgot to restock?"

He huffs out a laugh and then drops his head, but not before I see his cheeks deepen in color from embarrassment. "It's been a long time since I was with anyone. I haven't had a need for them."

"Oh."

"Yeah."

Our breaths even out and my heart rate starts to steady, but my body is still thrumming with need, and I can only imagine how worked up he is. I, at least, got a release.

"I know something we can do without condoms," I say.

# TWENTY-TWO

# Gabe

I'm my own fucking cock-block; I can't believe I don't have any condoms. I'm mentally beating myself up when Danae's husky voice says, "I know something we can do without condoms."

I pull my head up off her chest and look into her light-brown eyes. My cock jerks between us, desperate for her.

She places her small hands on my shoulders and pushes me up until I'm standing and she's sitting on the table. Then, with a graceful move that I will replay in my mind for years to come, she slides off the table and onto her knees, her eyes still connected with mine.

I swallow hard as she grips the waistband of my shorts and pulls them down until they drop to my ankles, and my thick erection bobs in front of her face. She grips my cock in her hand, and there's no way to fight back the groan that rips from my throat as her fingers squeeze.

The heated look she gives me would put any seductress to shame as she licks the head of my cock, never breaking eye contact. I can barely inhale as she licks me like I'm an ice cream cone and she's determined to savor every creamy drop. My fingers slide into her hair as she stops toying with me and takes me deep into her throat.

My entire body seizes up as I fight my impending orgasm—fear stiffening my spine because I don't want to come too soon and end this insane pleasure.

She hums around my cock as her hand slides up and down, gripping and twisting in a way that makes it hard to remember my own name. If she keeps this up, this will end way too soon. It's been too fucking long since I've had sex, and her mouth feels like heaven.

Gripping her hair, I try to get her to slow her movements. "D-Danae. God, sweetheart, I need you to slow down or I'm going to come."

She moans, but doesn't slow her pace. Instead, she takes me deeper until she's choking on my cock, then swallowing and letting her tight throat constrict around the head. With a shuddering roar, I pull back and hold the base of my cock as I come all over her beautiful breasts. She leans forward and licks my still-sensitive tip, and my body shakes. I drop my head back as I stroke the base of my cock, coming down from the best orgasm I've had in a long fucking time.

When I tilt my head to look down at her, she's already staring up at me with a coy smile like the cat that got the cream. "I think you sucked my soul out of my body," I murmur.

She tilts her head back and laughs, and it's such a carefree sound that my heart feels lighter in my chest. I want her to be that happy all the time.

"Come on, gorgeous. Let's go take a shower and clean up."

I pull her to standing, but before I move to take us upstairs, I slide my fingers into her hair and tilt her head back. I press my lips to hers in a sweet, tender kiss that I hope says all the things I don't have the words for. I don't know exactly where we're going from here, but I know we sure as shit aren't going backward. I can't fight my feelings for her anymore, not after this.

When we finally pull away from each other, her eyes gleam with affection. But I want to ensure there's no confusion about what exactly I want. I don't want a quick fuck or even a fuck buddy. I want so much more with her, but actions always speak louder than words, so I pick her up and carry her to my master bath. Without putting her down, I turn on the shower and then step inside with her in my arms. Her gaze is soft as I carefully place her down and then grab my shampoo and start washing her hair. Her eyes close as she lets out a soft hum and sways closer to me. I massage her scalp and then tilt her head back to rinse it in the hot water. Next I grab my body wash and, with careful precision, clean every inch of her perfect body. My blood heats when I notice small scars that dot her otherwise unblemished skin—evidence of the hell she's been through. After I rinse the soap away from each scar, I leave a tender kiss. The first one causes her to inhale sharply, but as I continue on and she realizes what I'm doing, it turns into soft moans.

When I make my way back up her body, she grabs my face and pulls my mouth to hers, kissing me so deeply I feel it in my soul. Does she have any idea how much I belong to her already?

With one last kiss, she pulls away and grabs my shampoo off the rack. "My turn," she says, giving me the same treatment I just gave her. I soak in her touch, the way her delicate fingers massage my scalp and then all the muscles on my body until we're both squeaky clean.

And yet, we still can't seem to stop touching each other.

After weeks of denial, I don't know that I'll ever want to stop.

⬤

The next morning when I roll over and stretch my arm across my bed, all I find are cold sheets. I sit up, glance at the clock on my nightstand, and then call out, "Danae?"

She doesn't respond, but if I strain to listen, I can faintly hear music playing somewhere downstairs. After snuggling on the couch for the rest of the evening yesterday, we ended up in my bed together, my big body holding hers as we made out like teenagers until we both fell asleep. It was the best night of sleep I've had in a long time.

I quickly throw on a clean pair of sweats and then follow the sounds coming from my laundry room. When I round the corner and glance inside, Danae is in the process of moving clothes from the washer to the dryer. Leaning my shoulder against the door frame, I admire the way her body moves, especially when she leans over the washer to grab the laundry detergent and the motion emphasizes her round, full ass. I bite back a groan and amble into the room, then quickly wrap her up in my arms when I reach her, her back nestled against my front. My lips drop to her shoulder where I trail kisses up to her ear and whisper, "What are you doing?"

She tilts her head to the side, granting me more access that I take full advantage of. Her voice is breathy when she speaks. "Laundry, but I thought that was obvious since we're in the laundry room."

"Yes, but why?"

Her brows are furrowed when she turns to face me,

wrapping her arms around my shoulders. "Because it's my job."

I hold her close and love how her body melts against mine. I want her to always be this relaxed. "Not anymore. I fired you, remember?"

Now she stiffens and pulls back to look at me fully. "You were serious about that?"

"Well...yeah."

Her furrow turns into a full-on frown as she pulls away from me completely. "So what am I supposed to do now?"

I shrug. "Anything you want."

She shoves frustrated hands through her hair as she looks at the ceiling. "You don't get it, Gabe. I need to work. I still have to build up my savings. I mean, what happened last night was amazing, but it doesn't change the fact that I have to..." She cuts off her speech.

"You have to what?" I ask, my voice carefully calm.

When she looks back at me, there's such defeat in her eyes, my stomach tightens with the need to fix it. "I have to be ready, Gabe. He'll find me. He always does."

I step closer. "He's not getting anywhere near you. I promise."

"That's not a promise you can make. I need a job. I need to make my own money and have some sense of purpose and know that if shit hits the fan or things don't work out with us, I didn't just rely on another man to take care of me. I'll never be okay with that after what happened with Mitch."

I cup her face delicately in my hands. "I'm not him, and I'm not going to stop you from being independent or doing whatever it is you want to do. I don't want you to work for me because you feel like you have to. I want you to pursue whatever you've always wanted. Nothing changes about your setup here. You'll still have a free place to live, although I hope you'll move to my room instead of living out in the pool house because I'm kind of addicted to the feel of you next to me while I sleep."

Her lips tilt up ever so slightly at the edges as she looks up at me from under thick black lashes. I brush my fingers through her hair, gathering my thoughts while I admire how fucking gorgeous she is.

"I don't want you to feel like a bird trapped in a cage anymore."

She nibbles her lip and lets out a sigh weighted with all the burdens she carries. I just wish she'd realize she doesn't have to carry them alone anymore. I don't want to hinder her or make her feel like she has to rely on me. I just want to help.

"I don't want to feel that way either, but I can't rely solely on you."

"Fair enough. What have you always wanted to do?"

# TWENTY-THREE

# Danae

No one has ever asked me that before. I've always just survived, even before Mitch. I got my first job working under the table at fourteen to help pay the bills. I've always done what I had to do, and not once did anyone ever ask me what I actually *wanted* to do.

"I could pay for you to go back to school if you want to get a degree or certification in something."

A degree definitely would've come in handy when it came to better paying jobs when I was on the run, but the problem with those is that they want references and there's no way an employer would give a glowing recommendation to an employee who just up and vanished one day.

"I have to think about it," I say. It's not that I'm opposed to his generosity or have concerns about taking him up on his offer to pay for school. It's because I honestly have no idea what I want to do. I gave up on the idea of dreams a long time ago.

"Okay," he says, his fingers still in my hair and his chest pressed lightly against mine. The warmth of his body seeps through me, comforting me from the mild panic that shot through me when I realized he'd been serious when he fired me yesterday. "So, where does that leave us?" he asks.

I glance up at him and for the first time see a hint of vulnerability in his eyes. This fierce, beastly man is staring at me like my answer will turn his whole world topsy-turvy. No one has ever looked at me the way Gabe Romero does.

"Where do you want it to leave us?"

He shakes his head. "Uh-uh. This is your call. I think you already know what I want, but I care more about what you want."

My heart squeezes at the truth in his eyes. If I told him right now last night was great, but I think we should be friends, that's what he'd do. I have no doubt.

But that's not what I want, and I don't know what scares me more—how freaked-out I should be by my already intense feelings for him, or how much I'm not freaked-out at all.

Making eye contact with him, I slide my palm up his bare chest until it rests over his racing heart. "I want you."

His head swoops down and his lips brush against mine while his arms wrap around my waist and pull me flush against his body. His erection is already prominent in his sweats, and I wish with desperation that he had a condom in this damn house.

I break the kiss. "You have to go to the store today and buy condoms. I need to feel you inside me." If I was on birth control, I'd say fuck it and tell him to go in bare, but I haven't been on birth control since I ran out of pills a month after I broke up with Mitch. It might be time to consider making an appointment with a doctor and going on something that has less daily maintenance than the pill.

He groans against my neck, his hips thrusting against my covered pussy. "Fuck," he murmurs, and then stands up straight and stares down at me. I can practically see the light bulb going off in his head.

He holds up a finger. "Wait right here for one minute."

He spins around and races out of the room, only to return a few minutes later with a jar of coconut oil in his hand and a *very* bashful look on his face.

"I thought you might've remembered you had a condom somewhere."

"No such luck, but...we could do something else."

I arch a brow. "I didn't think coconut oil was used as a contraceptive. I've always heard it used as lube."

He nods. "Lube was the direction my mind went."

"Okaaaay," I say. "But what's the point of lube if we don't have any condoms?"

"I wouldn't use it to fuck your pussy."

His vulgar words make my stomach clench and wetness flood my panties. And then they actually register and my mind completely short-circuits. "You...my ass?"

He nods, his face the picture of seriousness, and I bark out a laugh because he's acting like this is the most intense conversation he's ever had.

"I can't believe I didn't think of that. Clearly I'm out of practice."

He stares at me with hopefulness. "It doesn't freak you out?"

I tilt my head. "Why would it?"

He shrugs. "I don't know. Most women in my experience think it's gross or taboo or something."

I step forward and shift onto my tiptoes so I can place a light kiss to his lips. "I guess I'm not most women," I say and then spin around, pull my pants down, and bend over, resting my arms on the top of the washer.

Gabe's groan fills the room. "No, you sure as hell are

not." I feel his big body drape over mine, as he nuzzles my neck. "You're so much better than anyone else." His words are quiet, but their impact on me is strong.

This isn't my first time trying anal—far from it—but it's the first time I've been so excited for it.

Instead of getting started with the coconut oil, he drops to his knees and nibbles my ass cheek, first one, then the other, before kissing his way between my thighs. I stand on my toes and spread my legs farther apart to give him more room and am immediately rewarded when he starts eating me out from behind. My stomach flips as he shoves his tongue inside me as far as it will go, and tingles start to flutter in my clit.

I grip the edge of the washer. "Oh shit," I choke out as the pleasure builds, and he buries his face so hard against my slick folds that I'm convinced he's going to suffocate if he doesn't take a breath soon.

"Fuck, you taste so good," he murmurs before diving back for more.

"Gabe," I say, my voice taking on a desperate edge as my legs start to shake with my impending release, but he doesn't ease up. When he sticks his pinky inside my ass at the same time that he sucks hard on my clit, I scream, my orgasm pounding through me in blissful waves that make spots dance in my eyes.

"That's it. Let me taste every last drop," he says, licking me like I'm the best fucking thing he's ever eaten. My body sags against the washing machine, my breaths coming out heavy and my legs still shaking.

"I want you inside me."

He kisses his way up my back until he's holding his body draped over me. Instead of feeling suffocating, it feels protective, and I push back so we're touching completely. A soft moan escapes when I feel his stiff erection against my butt.

"Please," I beg.

He kisses my shoulder and then my neck, sending goose bumps down my arms at how good it feels.

"Fuck, I'm never going to get enough of you," he murmurs before spinning me around and kissing me fiercely. Our tongues lash against each other while we kiss each other senseless. He slides his hand down by body, pinching my nipple and eliciting a moan from me before sliding it down and moving two fingers inside my slick pussy. I grip his biceps as his fingers work inside me like they know every little spot to hit in order to send me over the edge again. My nails dig in as his biceps flex, and his talented fingers rip another earth-shattering orgasm out of my body.

He wraps an arm around my waist to hold me up as I collapse against him.

"Oh my God."

He kisses my cheek and jaw and neck before coming back to my mouth like he can't stop himself.

"Give me more," I say, eager to feel him buried in my ass, even after already coming twice.

He spins me around and gently pushes me down so my upper body is resting over the washing machine. Then he grabs the bottle of coconut oil and quickly takes off the lid. The smooth surface shows it's never been used, and in my head I'm already planning on moving it to his room so it'll only ever be used for bedroom stuff. He surprises me when he pulls a spoon from his pocket and scoops out a generous amount before moving it to his fingers. I don't know if I would've had the forethought to think about that in my sex-addled brain.

He spreads the coconut oil into my crack, pushing it in slowly with first his pinky and then his thumb.

Gabe's breathing turns heavy. "If you could see what I see right now..." His voice fades as he uses more oil on my ass. Then he sets the jar down and uses his free hand to rub soothingly on the middle of my back. It's so relaxing, I almost don't notice when he replaces his thumb with two fingers, and I suck in a sharp gasp.

"Fuck," he whispers, pushing his fingers all the way inside and stretching me to prepare me for the beast between his legs. It's uncomfortable, but not painful. The pressure is always a little strange at first, until it subsides and turns into pleasure. Although it's never felt quite as pleasurable as this.

He pulls his fingers out, and I peek back to see him shuck his sweats to the side, standing unabashedly naked behind me. I ache to touch him, but the fierce concentration on his face makes me think that might not be a distraction he's ready for. His big, warm hands slide up and down my sides. "You're so damn beautiful," he murmurs, leaning over to kiss between my shoulder blades.

Desire pulses heavily in my clit, but it's nothing compared to the intense affection that warms my chest and nearly overwhelms me.

And that's before he works his hard shaft inside me. He rubs the head of his dick against my tight puckered hole and then slowly eases his way in. The pressure is more intense than I'm used to and borders on the edge of pain. "Fuck, it's so tight," he says, his fingers gripping my hips.

He's going so slow, it's only causing the pressure to linger, and I'm ready for the pleasure. I push back on his cock, taking him the rest of the way inside in one swift shift.

The movement causes him to inhale sharply and let out a string of curses, but I'm too distracted by how full I feel.

"Oh God," I cry out, desperation for release clawing at me and causing my hips to have a mind of their own, rocking back and forth on his dick now that the pressure has subsided and all I feel is pleasurable bliss.

He makes an unintelligible sound behind me, and then the tether snaps and he thrusts deep, quickly finding a rhythm that leaves me breathless and spinning. One of his hands slides around to my stomach and then moves down until he's rubbing my clit while he pounds into my ass.

That's all it takes to tip me over. I come again with a scream as my orgasm rips through me, making me feel like I've been pulled apart and put back together again. Gabe growls behind me and then stills, and I can feel the pulse of his come as he releases inside me.

He collapses on my back, panting heavily. "Shit, woman. You've fucking ruined me."

I huff out a laugh as I try to catch my own breath. "The feeling's mutual."

It should feel weird to be so honest with him after so long of keeping everyone at arm's length, but it doesn't. It feels natural and so achingly effortless that I start to hope Gabe is right.

That he can keep his promise to keep me safe.

That he can keep *me*.

# TWENTY-FOUR

# Gabe

It's been a long time since I've taken a girl home to meet my family, and I'm still not sure it's a good idea because I'm afraid they're going to scare her off.

My family can be...intense. But when you add the extended relatives and throw them all together for my cousin's quinceañera, it's like a whole other experience.

"Tell me about your cousin," Danae says from the passenger seat of my car. I glance at her briefly before looking back at the road. We've been together as a couple for two weeks, and it still feels surreal. She's like all my greatest fantasies thrown together with a million things I never knew I wanted in a woman.

"Lily Rose. She was named after my aunt's two favorite flowers. All her daughters have the same middle name in fact. Lily, Eva, and Mari. Lily is the oldest and wants to go to school to be a doctor."

"What made her want to be a doctor?"

"I'm not really sure. There's a ten-year age gap between us, so we aren't that close. There are two sets of cousins in my family. My siblings and I are part of the first set, which are all the kids of my dad and his siblings. We're all in our twenties and thirties, but my mom was five years younger than my dad and she was the oldest, so her side of the family is the second set and they're mostly early teens and adolescents. Lily's the oldest of that set."

"And a quinceañera means she's fifteen, right?"

"Yup," I say, checking the lane next to me as I move toward our exit. "A quince is a huge deal in my family, and it's the one event where you can guarantee everyone will drop everything and attend. My aunt's been planning this for over a year and messaged me about my schedule probably close to a million times before dates were settled on. I might not be super close to her, but she's family. I'd never miss such an important occasion."

Danae's hand slides over my thigh and she gives it a gentle squeeze. "You're really sweet, you know that?"

I smile at her words, especially after our game yesterday where sports reporters were calling me a beast on the turf. "Shhh. You'll ruin my rep with that gossip."

She laughs and the sound fills the car and eases my tense muscles.

"Tell me more about your mom and sisters."

Cami stopped by the house a week ago and met her briefly, but I haven't told Danae much about my family apart from what I'd told her before we got together. Mainly because most of the time all I want to do is bury myself inside her or get her to open up and tell me all about herself after so long of not being able to pry for fear of making her nervous around me.

"You met Camila. She lives in LA and works as a personal assistant for a celebrity, but she refuses to tell us who it is. Ella is my little sister. She's still figuring out what she wants to do with her life."

"And you said she lives in San Diego?" she asks.

"Yeah, in a little bungalow near Coronado with two of her best friends. I've told her she's not allowed to fall for a navy guy."

"Seriously?"

"No, not seriously. Although I do worry that one of those guys is going to break her heart. Her friend Cara isn't the best influence and tends to go for guys for all the wrong reasons. I don't want Ella falling into that trap, which would be far too easy since she's already feeling so lost."

"Are you close to her?"

"Not as close as we used to be. When she was little, she came to me about everything. But these days...I don't know. It's harder. The older she gets the more she pulls away and the more I feel like a father figure nagging her to check in and less like her big brother who's genuinely worried about her. It's one of the reasons I'm happy to live so close. I mean, it's still a couple hours' drive, but that's better than living across the country, like I was my rookie year."

"Who did you play for?"

"Tampa Bay. I got traded to the Wolves after one season and have been there for three years now."

"I bet your mom loves that you're close," Danae says, with a wistfulness that makes me wonder if she's missing her own mom right about now.

"Yeah, she does. And we're really close, so I like being able to check in on her and make sure she's doing okay."

She squeezes my thigh again, right as I pull into the parking lot of the large venue where Lily is having her quince. "You're a good son," she says.

I put the car in park and then slide my fingers through her hair and pull her mouth to meet mine over the armrest.

This woman ties me up in knots, but I'm terrified that today might be too much for her.

I pull back and look into her gorgeous eyes. "My family means the world to me," I whisper. "And I know they're going to like you as much as I do." I withhold the other "L" word that I suspect is more accurate, but would freak her out. It's too soon, even if we have been dancing around our feelings for well over a month now.

She twists her lips. "Well, let's hope not *as much as* you, or that might get a little awkward when they try to kiss me."

A smile rips across my face before I throw my head back and laugh, deep, loud, and freeing.

This woman.

She's more than I ever could've hoped to find.

"Come on, let's get in there before my mom sends out a search party."

I get out and meet her on her side of the car, and then with her hand in mine, we make our way inside. The second we pass the door, I'm bombarded by relatives. Aunts, uncles, cousins, family friends who are honorary aunts and uncles, and my grandparents. It feels like they all converge on us at once, asking questions, some in English, but the pushier ones in Spanish, thank God.

*Who's this gorgeous girl?*

*What's her name?*

*How'd you two meet?*

*¿Cuándo se van a casar?*

*¿Cuándo vas a tener bebes?*

I can only imagine how fast she'd be out of here if she heard them asking when we're getting married and having babies.

"Alright! That's enough. Give the boy some room," a strong feminine voice yells from behind the crowd. I glance up from my abuela to see my mom standing next to my aunt, both of their expressions stern and their arms crossed. "Today is about Lily, so stop harassing Gabe and his guest," my mom adds and my anxiety eases. She's a small woman with a large personality and an even bigger heart.

Everyone grumbles—although none louder than my uncle who argues that he wanted to talk football, and quickly gets slapped on the arm by his wife—but disperses, heading toward the round tables bordering the dance floor. The room is extravagantly decorated in mixes of a deep pink and plum purple. Flowers are everywhere, but in a way that's sophisticated instead of chaotic. Having gone through the experience of watching my mom and aunts plan both my sisters' quinces, I know how much work went in to making sure no detail was overlooked.

"Woah," Danae says with clear awe in her voice as her eyes scan the room and take in every detail. "This is gorgeous."

"Yeah, they did a great job."

"Your family did all this?" When I nod, she continues, sounding even more impressed. "I bet they'd make a killing as event planners if they ever decided to go into business."

"There are a lot of girls in the family, and they do this for every single one."

"It's incredible." The hint of wistfulness I thought I heard in the car is subtle, but still in her voice, and I wonder if anyone's ever done anything this grand for her. Has anyone ever made her birthday special?

Or was the library I had built for her the first time someone put so much effort in for her?

Before either of us has a chance to say anything else, my mom moves closer to us, clearly done herding the rest of the family away. She comes up to me, spreading her arms out wide, and I instantly pull her into a hug as her strong arms wrap around my shoulders.

"Ay mijito, I've missed you," she says as she pulls back and then frowns. "Are they feeding you enough when you travel? You look too skinny."

No one but my mother has ever accused me—two hundred and thirty pounds of muscle in a six-foot-four frame—of being skinny. "Mamá, I eat six meals a day and snacks between. I eat more protein in a week than you probably eat in a month. Trust me, I'm eating just fine."

She mumbles something with a frown still marring her face, but then she turns to Danae, and it quickly spreads into a smile as she wraps her up in a hug. "You must be Danae!" She pulls back, holding Danae at arm's length before looking me dead in the eyes, an accusatory expression on her face. "You didn't mention how beautiful she was."

Danae's gaze drops to the floor, but the corner of her mouth tilts up and I know she's pleased—or embarrassed—by the compliment.

"Mamá."

She waves her hand at me as if to shush me and then locks her elbow with Danae's and starts moving toward the tables, assuming I'll follow. Which, of course, I do.

There's too much going on for me to catch everything that she says to Danae, but I watch the expression on her face fill with affection as she looks at my mother, and that warm, tingly sensation I get whenever Danae's around intensifies.

"How does that sound?" my mother asks as she stops at a table and pulls out a chair for Danae.

Danae smiles at her, a smile that reaches her eyes and

nearly makes my final steps stutter at how gorgeous she is. "I would absolutely love that, Mrs. Romero."

"Oh, call me Nina." My mom glances back at me and with a mischievous grin on her face, says to Danae, "You're practically family now."

With that, she places a kiss on Danae's cheek and then mine before hurrying off to help my aunt. I take a seat next to my girl and rest my arm across the back of her chair as I lean closer to her. "What was that about?"

"Your mom offered to come over and teach me how to make tamales."

I sit back slightly, trying to hide my shock. My mother was taught by her mother and taught all of us kids starting at an early age. It's become something of a family tradition, but she's never once taught a girl I was dating. It's not even that she does anything particularly special to make her tamales. It's the act itself that is significant, and that she's invited Danae to learn from her. I'm speechless and also so fucking thankful for my mom, that with just the little information I told her and one interaction, she was able to see how things are different with Danae and how serious we are.

Unfortunately, Danae misreads my shock and her smile drops. "Should I have told her no? Do you not want—"

I don't even let her go down that road. "No, no. Nothing like that." I gently grab her hands, holding them in mine. "I love that my mom wants to teach you how to make her tamales. They're my favorite."

"I know," she says, her smile slowly reappearing. "She told me."

Leaning forward, I place a tender kiss on her lips, loving the way her body relaxes closer to mine, and I can practically feel her anxiety melt away. The rest of the day goes by in a fog, my mind, body, and soul completely focused on Danae and how everyone she interacts with falls in love with her. My sisters both give me the thumbs-up when she turns away, and my mom makes multiple excuses to come sit with us, spending most of her time at our table talking with Danae instead of me. But I don't mind. Not when I can so easily picture our future—how seamlessly she fits with my family and my life.

And now I'm the one wanting to ask the invasive questions like weddings and babies and how soon I can commit myself to her in every way possible. There's no denying it any longer. She's my queen—the ruler of my heart.

*Mi Reina.*

TWENTY-FIVE

# Danae

"Come with me. I want to show you something," Gabe whispers in my ear, tugging me away from the celebration that shows no signs of stopping even though we've been here for hours.

Gabe's cousin Lily looks absolutely gorgeous in her ball gown-style dress. She looks like a fairytale princess if I ever saw one. The magic and ritual of this whole event has been so stunning and powerful, not to mention the impact of seeing such a devoted and loving family. More than once tonight, I've had to actively fight back the threat of tears.

Years of struggling and disappointments have taught me not to wish for things I can't have, but today, it can't be avoided. I want this. I want a family that comes together to spoil a girl rotten on her fifteenth birthday. I want a man who sits by my side and sees to my every need all night long. I want a mother who flits around from table to table, but always circles back and makes time for her children.

I want so many things that my head is spinning. It was only a couple of months ago when I thought I'd finally hit rock bottom and any semblance of a happy ending seemed out of the realm of possibility.

And now I'm here with a man who makes me feel special every day.

Who makes it easy to fall so much harder than I've ever fallen before.

Except...it doesn't feel like falling. Falling hurts. It causes scrapes and bruises, or worse.

That's not how Gabe makes me feel. He makes me feel light, like he's carrying me, and caring *for* me. There is no falling when it comes to Gabe, only flying, free as a bird in a cloudless sky.

His warm hand is wrapped around mine as he pulls me from the crowded hall and out the doors to his car. "Where are we going?" I ask.

He looks down at me, clear affection in his handsome brown gaze. "Somewhere special."

I don't pepper him with questions, but instead choose to trust that he'll keep me safe no matter where we go. He opens my door when we get to his car and then moves around the front to the driver's side. As soon as he gets the car on the road, his free hand moves to rest on my thigh in a hold that's both comforting and slightly possessive. I never thought I'd enjoy a man staking any kind of claim on me or my body after everything Mitch put me through, but I realize now it's more about the *right* man.

The setting sun highlights the beauty of San Diego as we make our way closer to the sandy beaches. He pulls to a stop in a quiet little neighborhood near a cluster of tall grass. When I turn to him, his dark gaze is already focused on me.

"Do you trust me?"

"Yes." It's a whisper, but there is no hesitation and that's what I hold on to. I do trust him. More than I've trusted anyone since my mom died.

He smiles and then gets out of the car, moving to the back this time and pulling something from the trunk. When he opens my door, he's got a thick blue blanket under his arm.

Without a word, I slide out of the car and then take his hand and let him guide me through the tall grass. Sand sneaks into my heels, and I pause to pull them off, carrying them in one hand and digging my toes into the soft sand with every step. The crashing of the waves gets louder the farther in we walk, until we break out of the grass and my mouth parts on a silent gasp.

Before me is a pristine tan sandy beach leading to a dark-blue ocean, and not another soul is in sight. The sun hovers above the horizon of the water, painting the sky in a jaw-dropping mix of orange, yellow, pink, and red hues. There's not a single cloud in the sky.

It's like we walked right into our own private beach oasis.

"How'd you find this place?" I ask.

"I grew up down the street. It's a neighborhood treasure that we tend to keep to ourselves."

"It's gorgeous," I say, looking at the rocky outcrop down to the right and the tall grass to our left.

"Yeah, I thought you might like it." He pauses, but his mouth opens and then closes like he wants to say something else.

"What?"

He looks down at me, his eyes piercing and the light from the setting sun highlighting the different shades of brown. "I've never brought a girl here."

Goosebumps lick across my arms and my legs, but I

don't bother to look at them. I'm too distracted looking at Gabe—the way his big chest moves up and down at a steady pace, the intensity of his eyes as they watch my reaction to his declaration, and his large hand that's still wrapped around mine.

I step in front of him, brushing my body against his, then use my free hand to tug on the buttons of his shirt until he smirks and then drops his mouth down to mine. The kiss starts out soft, playful, but it doesn't stay that way for long.

The moment his tongue licks across my lips, something shifts. The kiss turns deeper, bolder, stronger. My arms wrap around his neck while his wrap around my back and he pulls me tight against him. He lets out a groan that vibrates through my body and spikes my need for him.

Breaking the kiss, he leans back. With a smile, he says, "Hold that thought."

Pulling away completely, he picks up the blanket that fell to the ground beside him and quickly shakes it out and opens it on a patch of sand. He sits down, spreads his legs, and reaches out his hand. When I take it, he moves me to sit between his legs, my back to his front, so he can wrap his arms around me while we watch the waves break. Sitting in the cocoon of his arms, I've never felt safer or more cherished. My hands roam his pant-covered legs and then his arms, unable to stop touching him.

Caressing him.

Wanting him.

Loving him.

My breath catches, but it coincides with him kissing my neck, so he doesn't ask about it or realize the epiphany I just had—that I'm not falling for Gabe, I'm already in love with him.

As his lips continue their leisurely kisses on my neck,

his hand rubs the outside of my thigh, slowly moving up and pushing the loose material of my dress out of the way. My pulse pounds furiously as his fingers move closer and closer to where I need him, and I can't stop my hips from thrusting forward, eager to make contact.

He chuckles behind me. "Eager, mi reina?"

"Mi reina?"

"Hmm," is all he says, before his talented fingers rub my clit over my panties. I'm already soaked and the material is flimsy, but his fingers are just enough of a tease that I forget about asking him again what he said. When he pushes my panties off my body and slides his fingers inside, I forget everything except him, me, and the sound of the ocean as the backdrop to my moans.

His fingers thrust deeper and then he curls them at the same time that his thumb grazes my clit, and I explode with a gasp. His free arm wraps around me to hold me steady as his other hand keeps fingering my orgasm out of me until he's milked every last drop.

I relax back against him and look up at the stars twinkling brightly against the black night sky. The nearly fully moon shines brightly off the ocean water in front of us and lights up the beach just enough to be soothing and romantic.

Gabe continues to pepper kisses along my neck, but that's not enough for me. I want all of him.

Turning over, I get on my knees and unbutton his pants, pulling them down his body as he leans back on his hands and lifts his hips.

"Fuck, you're going to get me arrested for public indecency and it would so be worth it," he says as his large hands glide over the sleeves of my dress and pull down the loose material until my breasts are bared to him. His gaze turns hungry as he licks his lips and then leans forward, taking one pert nipple into his warm mouth while his hand squeezes my other breast. My head tips backward as my hands instinctively grab onto his hair, only for my gaze to shoot to his when there's a sharp tug on my nipple. He does it again, never breaking contact, and my stomach tightens from the painful need that he's building inside me.

My chest heaves with unsteady pants now, and I'm embarrassingly wet between my thighs. I readjust myself so I'm straddling his legs, and my sex brushes against his hard cock.

He lets out a hiss when my wet pussy slides smoothly across his bare cock, and the feeling is so divine, I do it again.

We've used condoms religiously, but I got on birth control pretty quickly when we started having sex. We'd be safe to go bare now, and instead of scaring me shitless like the idea should, it only turns me on more.

"I want to feel you inside me," I say, and then lean forward until we're so close my lips brush his as I whisper, "completely bare."

He groans and then kisses me hard, and any other words die on our tongues. We speak with our bodies as he grabs the base of his cock and positions it at my entrance, both of us watching as I slide down on top of him until my clit rubs along his pelvis. This position gives me a lot of control, and I use it to my advantage, slowing our movements and luxuriating in the way his thick cock fills me so perfectly. We grind our bodies together as we hold each other close, our breaths mingling and our tongues twirling together.

All the times we've had sex before have felt urgent. There's nothing urgent about this.

Gabe and I rock together in perfect harmony until, like the ocean behind me, the wave of our shared climax breaks and crashes against the beach. We're both shaking slightly as we come down from our orgasm, and it takes us several minutes before we pull ourselves together. My head rests on his shoulder while his fingers trace soothing circles on my back until I finally feel composed enough to sit up.

Our gazes lock and then a hush falls over us as Gabe stares at me and says, "Thank you for coming with me today, mi reina. You don't know what it meant to me to see you with my family."

My heart fills with peace and contentment. "There's nowhere else I would rather be," I whisper.

I lean forward and capture his lips with mine until my curiosity gets the better of me and I pull back. "What's mi reina mean?"

He brushes a loose hair away from my face, his gaze filled with something that almost looks like love as he says, "My queen."

# Gabe

I fight back a chuckle as Danae squirms in the seat next to me. She's been antsy ever since I blindfolded her and told her I have a surprise for her. It's a testament to how much she trusts me that she's going along with it.

"Are you going to tell me where you're taking me, or should I just pretend I'm being kidnapped?" she asks, a smile on her face to let me know she's teasing.

"We're almost there. Just a few more minutes," I say as I take one of the last few turns to our destination.

I park and then get out of the car and run over to her side, eager to see her reaction to the surprise. I take her hand and guide her until we get to the beginning of a long walkway. When I pull away the blindfold, she blinks a few times, her eyes adjusting to the light, and then squints when she sees all the booths lining the walkway.

"What is this?" she asks, a faint smile on her face while her eyes are filled with confusion.

"It's a job fair. The college hosts it a few times a year, most often in the spring, but I saw a post about it happening now for winter graduates."

"A job fair?" She looks around again at the booths.

"Yeah, so you can get some ideas for what you might want to do instead of working for me." She doesn't seem as excited about this as I am, but that's okay. I'm sure she's just surprised. "They have a ton of different career fields, and the college even has a couple of tables that explain what degree or coursework you might need to get that job. I figured it's a cool way to see all your options in one place."

She opens her mouth but then closes it without saying anything. Almost like she's at a loss for words. "I know it's probably a lot to take in," I say, trying to see it from her perspective. There are at least fifty booths with various businesses for all of the different professions represented today. It's definitely overwhelming and a little daunting if I'm honest. Fuck, I'm glad I never had to go to one of these things for myself.

Football is all I've ever wanted to do. Math was easy, and I loved computers so getting a Computer Science and Math degree was a no-brainer, even if I knew I wasn't likely to use it for at least a decade if I was lucky. I can't imagine what it's like not knowing what you want to do with your life, or how terrifying that must be to just be...existing, adrift in your life with no direction.

Maybe I should've reached out to Ella and had her come too. She's still floundering trying to figure out what she wants to do with her life. Maybe this would've been easier for Danae if she had someone else with her who was in the same boat.

When she still doesn't say anything, I place my hand gently on her lower back. "Should we look around?"

"Sure," she says, but she doesn't sound sure at all.

"Is there any particular career you've ever been interested in? Maybe when you were younger?"

She glances up at me and nibbles her lip. "I was convinced I wanted to be a baker, but I can't bake very well —something I learned the hard way. It's all the measuring and precise amounts of ingredients. I'm better at cooking, but it's not something I want to do for a job."

"Hmm, well, what about a job that lets you read—maybe a librarian or something."

"I tried to get a job at a library in Seattle, but they required a library science degree."

I stop in my tracks and face her. "Wait, there's an actual degree to become a librarian?"

She arches a brow at me and huffs out a laugh. "Yeah, Gabe. It's not as simple as just liking books and knowing the Dewey decimal system. Librarians don't get nearly enough credit for all the work they have to do. The branch I visited in Seattle even had to deal with doing some of their own janitorial work because of budget cuts."

"I had no idea." I feel a little stupid now, and it's been a long time since I felt like a dumb jock, but when your whole life revolves around one thing, that tunnel vision means you rarely focus on the details of other professions.

We pass several booths and with each one, Danae's shoulders seem to grow more tense. "If this is too much, we could always audit a class or something instead. I just thought this would be a good way to see all your options, but I don't want you to feel overwhelmed."

She looks around before grabbing my hand and pulling me to the side, out of the way of the people milling around and talking to prospective employers. "I'm still not really sure what I want to do or what I'm interested in. It's not that I don't know what's out there. It's that I've been focused on surviving for so long it's hard to just change that mindset. It's not something I can just turn off like flipping a switch."

She squeezes my hand like she's reassuring me, when I feel like I should be the one reassuring her. "I appreciate what you're trying to do, but yeah, this is a bit overwhelming and not what I was expecting today. I'll figure it out. I just need a little more time, okay?"

"Yeah, that's fine. I just want you to know I'll support whatever you want to do. You said you needed something that gave you purpose, and I want that for you."

I want her to have everything she's ever wanted.

"I know you do, but could we maybe just go out for lunch today instead of doing more of this?" she asks, gesturing to the booths.

"Yeah, whatever you want."

Except as we make our way back to the car, there's a tension emanating from her that wasn't there before, and I start to wonder if I fumbled this whole situation. I'm used to taking care of things, getting things done. I want Danae to be happy and confident in her options, but more than that, I want her to be confident in *us*.

# TWENTY-SEVEN

# Danae

The next night, Gabe takes me to another open mic night—fortunately not at the same bar where we met—to see Emma perform again. It's different being a part of their group instead of looking on from the outside. All the women I met at the game are there with their guys sitting at the table next to us, and Ty also shows up.

"Romel opted to stay home with Kay. Said she wasn't feeling that great and he didn't want to leave her with a sitter," Ty says as he takes a sip of his beer.

"Where's Dom tonight?"

"Don't know. Probably hanging with Alayna."

I'm about to ask who Alayna is when Emma gets on stage, and just like before, I'm absolutely mesmerized by her stage presence. She sings with such heartfelt emotions that they practically flow through her over the audience. A single tear slides down her cheek when she closes her eyes and belts out a note that gives me goose bumps. It's emotional, raw, and beautifully haunting.

When she finishes, the audience claps wildly, and she

thanks them all with a blush staining her fair cheeks as she makes her way down the stairs and straight into the arms of her fiancé, Luke. He kisses her like no one else is watching, and when she pulls away, her blush looks like it's for a completely different reason.

My own cheeks heat as I look away and my gaze meets Gabe's, a knowing smirk on his handsome face. He wraps an arm around me, pulling me close, and I melt against him as he drops a kiss to my head that both turns me on and makes me feel cherished. There's been an awkward tension between us since he took me to the job fair yesterday, but it's not present right now. Instead, I feel the same security I always feel in his arms.

Emma walks over to our table, Luke's hand wrapped firmly around hers and his gaze watching her every move like she's the only person that exists in this bar.

"Thank you so much for coming," she says, leaning over and hugging me with her free arm.

"Are you kidding? I wouldn't have missed it. I still remember the last time I heard you perform. You're incredible up there."

She blushes again and then rolls her eyes. "Ugh, curse of the redhead. My freaking complexion gives me away every time. Thank you for saying that though. It means a lot to me." She glances at my almost empty glass, then up at Luke and Gabe. "You guys want to get more drinks for your ladies?"

They both grin but take the hint and head to the bar, taking Ty with them and leaving us to talk.

"Seriously, thank you for saying that about my music. It's not easy being an artist, and it certainly wasn't an easy road to get here, but hearing that even one person is touched by my music makes it all worth it."

"The first time I heard you sing, I literally couldn't look away. It felt so raw and real." I nibble my lip and debate asking her something I've wondered since that first night. But part of building friendships means being willing to actually open up and let people in, so I take a deep breath and ask. "It sounded like you'd been really hurt before. Was that based on a real experience?"

She stares at me for a minute, her eyes seeming to look into my soul. "I'm of the philosophy that the best art comes from releasing the feelings you get from real experiences, even if it's painful to relive it again. You never know who might feel a little less alone by hearing your truth. So, yes, I've been hurt before, both physically and emotionally, but I think we all have in some way or another. Some worse than others."

She doesn't ask me anything, but there's an unspoken question that lingers in the silence between us and I can't deny I want to open up to her. "Yeah, I, uh, know a little something about that."

Her voice is so soft when she speaks again, I have to lean forward to hear her. "I was broken for a long time after I was assaulted by a producer."

My hand automatically reaches out to hers. "Oh God, Emma. I'm so sorry, I had no idea."

She gives me that kind, compassionate smile I've come to expect from her. "How could you? It's not really something I talk about, except in my music. If you pay attention to the lyrics, you'll pick up on it."

I believe her, and wonder if that's why I've been so drawn to her songs—why they've had such an impact on me.

"It really messed with my head and my confidence," she continues. "It didn't help that things with me and Luke also got messed up when I was still doubting myself. It took a long time and a lot of therapy to work through it all. I couldn't write songs or sing hardly at all. For a long time, I felt like I was floundering, and had no idea what I wanted to do with my life anymore."

"I can relate to that," I say, then glance back to see Gabe still waiting at the busy bar. "Gabe recently asked me what I want to do with my life. The problem is, I have no idea. Yesterday, he took me to a job fair, and I feel like I disappointed him because it was all so overwhelming for me, and it made me feel like I was letting him down somehow by not knowing what career I might be interested in."

She's already shaking her head in dismay as I finish. "Oh my God, these boys can be so dumb sometimes. Here's the thing about professional athletes—their sport is all they know. They've lived and breathed the game for so long, they forget that normal people aren't always that driven or focused. They can be, but most take a while to figure out their passions and what they're good at. I read a statistic that said people have, like, seven different careers in their lifetimes—*careers*, not just jobs, so they could end up having way more jobs before they stumble on a career they're happy with. But for these guys, football is all they know and they just expect it to be that way for everyone else too. Don't be afraid to tell him what you need and call him out when he's being pushy. It's good for them to be called out from time to time."

I can't help but chuckle. "Noted."

She grabs my hand. "Come on. Let's go visit with the other WAGs and forget about overbearing boys."

I arch a brow. "WAGs?"

"Wives and girlfriends," she says.

"I have never heard that term before."

Emma laughs. "I have to confess, I'd never heard of it

either, but it's apparently very common in athlete circles." She leans in conspiratorially as we move over to the other table where Paige, Gina, and Nikki are sitting, their guys heading to the bar to refill their drinks. "I consider Paige the Queen Bee WAG whether she knows it or not because she's always so put together and knows everything that's going on. She's kind of amazing."

"I'm starting to think you all are amazing," I admit, which causes Emma to smile even wider.

"We think you're pretty awesome too. I'm so excited Gabe found someone nice. I always worry that one of the guys is going to start dating some bitchy woman who's a gold digger or something and ruin the great vibe we've got going on in our group."

"They definitely have no shortage of women to pick from, do they?"

She squeezes my arm, as if reassuring me. "But they only pick the best."

"Hey Emma?"

"Yeah?"

"Thanks for welcoming me into the group and being so inviting. I've never really had girlfriends before, and it's kind of nice."

She laughs. "You say that now, but wait until we have a girls' night and you have to listen to us talk about all sorts of crazy things."

"You mean like comparing the guys' dicks?"

She throws her head back, letting out a hearty laugh which only causes me to laugh too. Just then Gabe, Luke, and Ty rejoin the group with drinks for Emma and me in hand. The more we talk with the other girls, the more nothing sounds better than girls' nights with these ladies.

Except maybe going home and crawling into bed wrapped up in Gabe's strong arms.

That sounds like the best thing in the world.

# TWENTY-EIGHT

# Gabe

The sound of my phone ringing wakes me up. I reluctantly pull away from where I'm wrapped around Danae and reach for my phone resting on my nightstand. When I see my little sister's name on the display, I don't hesitate to answer.

"Hey," I say groggily, trying to keep my voice low so I don't wake up Danae. "Give me one sec."

"Sorry if I woke you. You're usually up by now," she says as I throw my sweats on and then leave the room, clicking the door shut quietly behind me.

"We had a late night out with some of the guys from the team and their girls." I don't mention how the night went even later when we got home and I fucked Danae against the door, then again in our bed—and it's definitely *our* bed now.

"So, what's up?" I ask.

"Are you free for breakfast? I volunteered to pick up a part for Lou and am about thirty minutes away from you."

"Who's Lou again?" I ask, rubbing my eye. It's so hard to

keep up with the people in her life when I'm not living down there.

"He's the mechanic that owns the garage I work at."

"Since when do you know anything about cars?"

I swear I can hear her eye roll, even if I know that's not possible. "I don't work on the cars. I work in their office and help with the customers."

"How long have you worked there?" I genuinely can't recall her ever mentioning this job before.

"Are you just going to judge my job choice, or are you going to get off your high horse and tell me where you want to meet for breakfast?"

"Meet me at Shay's. I'll be there in twenty and grab a table for us."

"Great, see you then." She hangs up and I rush up the stairs to change. I jot down a note in case Danae wakes up while I'm gone—she looks too peaceful to wake up—letting her know where I'll be and that I'll bring her back some breakfast. Hopefully we can eat it in bed and then I can eat her again.

My mouth waters at the thought. I love watching her come, but feeling her come—on my mouth, my fingers, my cock, it doesn't matter—is like experiencing heaven on earth.

I shake the naughty thoughts away and change into jeans and a T-shirt, then grab my keys and wallet and head out the door. The drive to my favorite breakfast joint is quick, and I get a table in the back where it's a little more secluded and I'm less likely to get asked for autographs. The Fierce Four have gained a lot of popularity in the last year or so, and when your face is plastered all over billboards during the season, it means a greater chance of getting noticed in public. The benefit of living in LA is that most people don't care. They're used to celebrities, so it's not a big deal to see someone famous—or semifamous like me—out and about. But I'd still rather be safe than sorry, so I can focus on my sister.

Ella arrives twenty minutes later looking a little frazzled. "Sorry, that took me longer than I expected because I couldn't find parking."

"You're good," I say, standing up to give her a hug before she takes her seat across from me.

"So, you're working for a mechanic?" I ask.

Her shoulders immediately sag and she huffs. "Can you not today, please?"

"What?" I ask, holding up my hands and at a complete loss for why she seems so annoyed with me.

"Look, I get that you think less of me because I'm not as driven as you, but your overbearingness about it is one of the reasons I don't talk to you much anymore. I just want to enjoy a nice breakfast with my brother without being criticized for my life."

I have to blink twice to convince myself that I'm actually sitting in a restaurant across from my five-foot-seven, one hundred and twenty-pound little sister and not flat on my back on the field after getting hit by a giant linebacker.

"What the hell are you talking about?"

"Are you serious, Gabe? Every single time I've seen you since I graduated from high school, you've been all over me about 'what I'm planning to do with my life,'" she says, using air quotes.

"Why is that a problem?"

"Because it's always asked with judgment in your tone, like the fact that I have no idea what kind of career I want means my life is unfulfilled. But it's not, Gabe. I'm happy with my life. I like my job. I like where I live. I like my friends. I don't need some big, fancy career like you do. I'm okay with being flexible, and if something isn't enjoyable anymore, I find something else. Yet, you always act like that's a bad thing and you get pushy about me finding something that you deem more worthwhile."

"I..." I stop myself. What she's saying makes me think about how Danae reacted when I took her to the job fair.

"I didn't realize I was doing that," I murmur, feeling smaller than I have in my entire life. "I don't mean to be overbearing. I just want the best for you."

"I know you do, but I hate to break it to you—you do it in a really overbearing and judgmental way. You're also really skilled at making me feel guilty about my choices, even when I know I shouldn't be, and I don't feel that way any other time."

"Fuck," I mutter before resting my elbows on the table and dropping my head into my hands. "I hope that's not how Danae feels."

Ella sits up taller, concern clear in her voice. "What did you do?"

"I fired her when we got together. I didn't want to be in a weird boss and employee dynamic, but she said she also needed to be self-sustaining. I've been letting her work still and paying her while encouraging her to try different things that she might be interested in."

"Oh, Gabe," she says, already shaking her head.

"I took her to a job fair at a local college and she seemed really overwhelmed, but now I'm wondering if she's feeling like you feel, which is the last thing I want for her."

"Okay, I'm going to drop a truth bomb that's been a long time coming." She leans forward on the table and pierces me with her gaze. "You got lucky. You figured out early on what you were good at and what you wanted to do with your life, and you had the drive to throw yourself completely into that. But that's not how it works for most people. Let Danae figure out her own life, and just be there to cheer her on as she does—that's the only support she needs. She doesn't need you to push job fairs, or classes, or career brochures on her. She'll figure it out."

"Just like you have," I say. Looking at her sitting across from me, it's clear she's more confident in herself than I remember her being when we were growing up.

"I wouldn't say I've figured it out, but I'm happy, and at the end of the day, that's what matters most to me. And it's more than some people can say."

"Yeah, I suppose you're right. I'm sorry for making you feel bad. I want you to be able to talk to me and share what's going on in your life."

"Even if it's about going to bars with Cara to meet lots of navy men?" she asks, but her eyes light mischievously and I know she's just messing with me.

"Even then," I say, and then we both break into laughter.

Breakfast is quick and uneventful after that, but a niggling feeling burrows in my gut, and by the end of it, I'm antsy to get home to Danae and clear the air.

No one gets to make her feel less than ever again, not even me. *Especially* not me.

I want to be her safe haven, not another man who makes her doubt herself. She's had enough of that for a lifetime.

Grabbing the breakfast I bought for her, I rush home.

# TWENTY-NINE

# Danae

I'm curled up in bed reading one of the romance novels that Gabe bought for me when I hear the door downstairs open and his hurried footsteps as he comes up the stairs. I sit up, a smile already tugging at my cheeks as he storms into the room, a to-go bag that smells divine in his hand and a determined expression on his face.

"I don't care what you do for a job."

My eyes widen and I shake my head. "What?"

"The job fair was too pushy, wasn't it? That's why it felt weird between us the rest of the day."

I open my mouth to respond, but he continues, starting to pace along the end of the bed as he talks. "I didn't realize I was being overbearing until Ella called me out for doing it to her." He stops and faces me. "I don't want you to think I'm forcing you to find a career path or making you feel less than because you don't know what you want to do. I was genuinely trying to help, but I'll stop."

I laugh—because what else do you do when your giant footballer boyfriend is having a hysterical meltdown in front of you. "Gabe, come here." I pat the bed next to me, and he comes and sits down, his face a mask of defeat. I can only imagine how many times his mother let him off the hook for something because of how adorable he looks with that expression on his face. Take twenty years off him and it would've been impossible to do anything but wrap him up in a hug.

"It's funny you're bringing this up now because Emma just told me last night that I needed to call you out when you were being too pushy."

"You told Emma?"

"It kind of came up organically. Does that bother you?"

"No," he says, his tone sincere as he grabs my hand. "I'm glad you're getting closer to her. I like you finding your place in my circle of friends."

I lean forward and kiss him before pulling away. "I know you have good intentions, Gabe. You've made that clear from the very beginning. But to answer your earlier question, yes, you can sometimes be a bit too pushy. I'm not entirely sure what I want to do, but Emma said something to me last night that's gotten me thinking and ruminating on an idea. I'll tell you more once I'm feeling more confident about it."

He leans forward, resting his forehead on mine. "Take Emma's advice and call me out anytime I get like that, okay?"

"I promise," I whisper.

His shoulders relax as if a weight has been removed but we remain close together, breathing each other in.

I point to the bag on the bed. "Is that for me by chance?"

He smirks. "Yeah."

"Good, because it smells delicious and I'm ravenous."

I reach for the bag, but he moves it away from me.

Before I can say a word, he opens it up and gets everything prepared, pouring the small container of syrup over warm blueberry pancakes that are covered in melted butter. He scoops up a piece of pancake and brings the fork to my mouth. My gaze locks on his as I open my mouth and he feeds me. I watch his every movement as he continues to feed me the entire pancake piece by piece. With each bite, my hunger for something completely different from food grows.

His eyes heat as he feeds me another bite and watches me chew and swallow. When he brings the next forkful toward my mouth, he tips the fork over so slightly and we both stare at each other as the bite drops between my sheet-covered legs.

"I better grab that," he says, his voice husky. But it's not his hand that reaches for the piece of food. Instead, he dips his head down, burying it between my legs as he picks up the pancake with his teeth. My heart is racing as he brings it to my mouth. When his teeth release it, he surges forward, pushing it inside a little with his tongue. The sweet maple syrup combined with the tang of the blueberries is nothing compared to the taste of Gabe. He doesn't linger long, pulling back and allowing me to chew, but the food does nothing to satiate my craving for him.

He smirks as he dips a finger in the maple syrup left over and then brings it toward my mouth. At the last second, he slides that finger from my bottom lip down my jaw.

"Oops," he says, his eyes heating as he leans forward and licks the maple syrup off me. I grip the sheets as I fight back a moan.

"Fuck, you taste delicious. I could eat you all day."

"Please do," I murmur.

"Your wish is my command," he says before once again dipping his finger into the syrup and then smearing it over my chest and between my breasts. The sheet I had pulled up to cover me falls, exposing my naked breasts. He doesn't hesitate to get more maple syrup and cover my nipples before sucking them into his mouth. He hums in pleasure and then bites down just enough to elicit a sharp gasp from me as my body starts to tremble.

"Gabe," I whisper, his name both a prayer and plea. "Please don't stop."

*Don't ever stop.*

He sits up, pulling the sheet completely away from my body and exposing my nakedness to his hungry eyes. He licks his lips and then pushes the tips of two fingers through the syrup in the to-go container before tracing between my breasts down my stomach until he reaches the apex of my thighs.

My chest constricts as his gaze connects with mine. Never looking away, he dips his head down and licks it from my body.

My nerve endings are buzzing as he reaches over and grabs more syrup, covering my pussy. He glances up at me, his eyes filled with heat and desire, and then devours me. I fall back against the bed, my fingers sliding into his hair and holding his head to my pussy while he eats me out. My legs shake and my stomach tightens as my orgasm builds. Then he shoves two fingers inside me, and that's all it takes to tip me over.

I sit up on my elbows while Gabe licks whatever maple syrup might've been left. He looks so hot with his mouth wet from my release and his brown eyes dark and filled with need. A beat passes and then both of us surge forward, colliding in a kiss. I can taste myself on him, and combined with the sweetness of the syrup, it's a heady mix of naughty and delicious. My hands roam, desperately trying to get him undressed as my tongue licks into his mouth and he lets out a deep groan.

"I need more," he says.

I spread my legs wide, allowing room for his body to nestle comfortably between my legs, and he hums with approval before kissing me again, softer this time, but no less needy. I drop back, resting my head against the pillow, and Gabe's hulking body cages me against the mattress. I should feel scared, or intimidated at the least. In the grand scheme of things, we haven't known each other that long. And yet, I'm more sure than I've ever been that Gabe will never hurt me.

I lift my head, needing to kiss him, and he meets me halfway, kissing the breath from my lungs as he guides the head of his dick between my pussy lips and then slowly pushes in. I inhale sharply as he stretches me wide to take his thick cock. Wrapping my legs tight around his waist, I cross my ankles at the base of his back, and then tilt my hips, urging him to move.

He doesn't need any more prompting than that, thrusting in and out of me at such a rapid pace that it doesn't take long for my legs to start shaking and a scream to rip out of my throat as my orgasm slams into me with brutal force. Two more pumps and he groans as he comes inside me, his upper body shuddering with a shiver before he collapses. He's careful to fall to the side instead of putting all his weight on top of me, but he still holds me close as he starts to soften and then slips out of me.

Neither of us move to clean ourselves up. Instead, he nuzzles my neck before placing a tender kiss on my shoulder. We lie like that for a while before finally getting up and showering together. He cleans me from head to toe, continuing to make me feel like I'm precious and deserve to be cared for.

A sense of belonging washes over me as he rinses us off and then wraps me in a big fluffy towel. He pulls me into his embrace and I close my eyes, letting my contentment seep into every inch of my body.

This right here is where I was always meant to end up. Now I just need to make sure nothing gets in the way of my first real chance at a happily ever after.

# THIRTY

# Gabe

This is insane. Dom has truly outdone himself this time.

Danae's eyebrow arches as she stands next to me and takes in the scene. "This is for his birthday?"

I shake my head as I see the outrageousness from her perspective. I'm used to Dom's antics, but this is definitely taking it to another level. He's rented out an entire warehouse and turned it into a glow-in-the-dark nightclub slash foam party. One-half of the room has a dance floor, bar, tables, and a DJ, while the other half has the largest inflatable pool I've ever seen that's filled with foam and girls in bikinis. Our single teammates are already down to their boxers as they "dance" with the women, although dance is a very loose term for the gyrating they're doing while they try not to lose their balance and slip.

"I don't think Dom knows how to do low-key."

"No kidding," I hear from behind me and turn to see Romel. "This is by far the craziest party he's thrown. I thought you were supposed to mature with age."

"Yeah, I think Dom missed that memo."

He looks around. "Where's Alayna? She usually keeps him under control."

"Who's Alayna again?" Danae asks me.

"His bestie from college...or high school maybe? I can't remember, but they've been best friends forever. I don't know how she puts up with him all the time."

She arches her brow at me again, and fuck if I don't love when she looks at me like that. "Don't you guys have to put up with him too?"

"Yes and no. When he gets too outrageous, we call him out, and if that doesn't work, we ignore him until he pulls his head out of his ass."

"Ah! There she is," Romel says just as a tall, curvy blonde walks through the crowd with a glare at the foam pit. "Alayna," he calls out, catching her attention.

She walks over to us and gives him a hug first, then me, and then smiles at Danae. "Hey, you must be Danae. I've heard a lot about you."

Now it's my turn to arch a brow, which causes her to roll her eyes. "If you think Dom keeps anything a secret from me, you're delusional. He said you'd met a lady and weren't any fun anymore, which I took to mean you were happy and didn't want to hang out with his degenerate ass anymore."

I fight back a smile. "That about sums it up."

She smiles back. "I'm happy for you, Gabe."

Then she turns to Danae. "Want all the dirt on these boys?"

Danae smiles wide. "Oh, definitely. Let's get drinks and you can fill me in."

"I like her already," Alayna says with a wink at me.

Then she ushers Danae away, and I watch helplessly as

I'm left with Romel. So much for finding a dark corner and fingering her until she comes all over my hand.

"You seen Ty?" I ask.

Romel shakes his head. "Nope. I saw Matt and Luke with their ladies, but only a handful of our guys." He looks around, a slight frown marring his face. "You know, this might be the first party of Dom's where I hardly know anyone. Well, wait. There's Coach," he says, pointing to a side bar where Coach Fairbright stands with her boyfriend or fiancé, Daniel. I'm not quite sure what their official status is now, although I have no doubt if he's not proposed yet, he will soon.

It's not all that strange that she's here. Dom usually invites everyone except Head Coach Denton—who wouldn't come anyway—to his parties. Coach Fairbright always drops in to make a quick appearance, but she looks just as lost at this party as Romel and I do. We make our way over to her, and she immediately lights up at the sight of friendly faces.

"Oh, thank God, people I know. I was starting to wonder if I'd stumbled on the wrong event. Dom's parties are always over-the-top, but this seems...like a lot, even for him."

"That's what I said too," Romel says before he reaches out to shake Daniel's hand. "Good to see you again, man."

Daniel smiles at him. "Yeah, you too." Then looking back and forth at both of us, he continues, "You guys played great the other night. The Championship is yours."

Coach immediately slaps him across the chest. "You can't jinx it like that! Don't you know anything about sports?"

He smiles at her and then glances back at us. "I love getting her fired up."

"You're impossible," she mumbles, but she can't hide the smile forming on her face.

We catch up with them for a while before she finally looks around. "Has anyone seen Dom? I wanted to wish him a happy birthday, but we have to head out soon."

"This was more of a drive-by," Daniel adds. "I'm on shift tomorrow."

Romel and I both look around. "We were wondering that too before we saw you. I haven't seen Ty either," I say.

"I think that's Ty right there," Romel says, pointing to a man currently being straddled by a bikini-clad woman while he sits on a chair near the foam pit.

"Yep, that would be our missing teammate."

"So now we just need to find Dom," Romel murmurs, and the four of us scan the room, but between the flashing black lights, the crazy foam bubbles floating into the air, and the hundreds of random people all over the place, it's impossible to spot him.

When Alayna finally returns with Danae, I ask her, "Have you seen Dom?"

She glances around the room. "I saw him when we got here, but I haven't seen him since things really started picking up. I thought he was near the foam pit last time."

"Wonder if he hooked up with someone," I say.

"I'll text him," Alayna says, pulling her phone out of the pocket in her dress and then moving her fingers over the screen faster than I've ever seen. When her fingers stop moving, she stares at the screen for a minute, but I can tell the instant he texts her back because her face immediately turns stormy.

She clenches her jaw and then looks up at the rest of us. "He...uh, he bailed. Said he had an opportunity he couldn't pass up."

I notice her voice catches at the end, and I wonder if he said something else, but decide not to push it.

"Well, if the birthday boy isn't even here, we're going to head out," Coach says.

"Yeah, I will too. I'd rather be home with Kay anyway. Now I can let the babysitter go early."

I glance down at Danae. "Want to stay or head home?"

"This isn't really my scene, so I'm happy to go home."

Thank God. This isn't my scene either, and maybe it makes me an old fuddy-duddy, but now that I have Danae in my life, I'd much rather spend my nights snuggled on the couch with her than out on the town. I get why the other committed guys on our team rarely come out to these things.

We've all had our wild times, but there's nothing like coming home to someone who you can let your guard down with and just be yourself.

"Alright, let's head out then."

We all say our goodbyes and then leave. In the car, I ask Danae, "So, what dirt did Alayna tell you?"

She chuckles. "She told me about how you guys secretly warm up to Taylor Swift."

My shoulders stiffen. That sonofabitch! That was supposed to be a secret we take to our graves. Imagine if the media found out one of the biggest, baddest, toughest defensive lines in the league were Swifties?

Jesus. It would be a public relations nightmare. I can only imagine the insults that would get slung our way when we're on the field. Even if she does have catchy tunes.

Squeezing the steering wheel and trying to find my chill, I ask, "What else did she tell you?"

I catch her shrug. "Not much. We mostly got to know each other. She said she's normally at the games when she can make it, but had a work obligation the day I was there. Apparently I got the seal of approval from the other ladies."

That doesn't surprise me. The LA Wolves' WAGs are a welcoming bunch. I've never met one who wasn't kind, except for maybe Ty's ex.

"So no more dirt on me then?"

She leans her head back on the seat rest and watches me with a soft smile on her face. "Is there a particular secret you don't want me to know?"

The fact she says it with a smile and not with worry makes me warm all over. She trusts me, and I vow never to jeopardize that trust. "You know you can ask me anything, and I'll answer honestly. I have no secrets from you, reina."

"Alright, then give me the dirt on Dom and Alayna."

I furrow my brow. "What do you mean?"

"How come they aren't a couple?"

"Probably because she's too smart and capable to be dragged down by Dom's craziness."

"Hmm."

She says it like she thinks there's more to the story. If there is, I don't know it. But I do know something I'll share with her. "Dom wasn't always like this."

"Like what exactly?"

I nibble my lips trying to organize my thoughts. "Out of control and inconsiderate. It's gotten significantly worse in the past two seasons. There's a rumor that Denton's one bad scandal away from kicking Dom off the team or forcing Fair-bright to bench him. But it's not widely spread. I'm not sure if Alayna met him now if she'd even be friends with him, but there's a loyalty there that a guy like Dom should appreciate."

"But he doesn't."

Her words hurt. Dom is one of my brothers, but I also

can't argue against it. Even I can see he's spiraling and getting more out of control as time goes by. I don't know how to help him, but more than that, I'm worried his actions are going to bring down our whole team.

This close to the playoffs, we can't afford to be as reckless as he's become.

"Sorry," she murmurs. "I didn't mean to talk bad about your friend."

There's a waver in her voice that has my gaze snapping to her. Her shoulders are hunched and her hands are bunched in her lap. Ice spreads down my spine and I reach out and grab her hand.

"You never have to apologize for sharing your opinion. I love hearing what you have to say and that you're comfortable enough with me to share it. And in this case, you're spot-on. I don't know what's going on with him and that worries me. That's why I got quiet. I'm not mad at you."

She closes her eyes, and her eyebrows squish together as her mouth pinches in frustration. "Sorry. I've had so many good days with you. I hate how this feeling of insecurity comes out of nowhere."

I squeeze her hand lightly. "You're a survivor of domestic abuse. It's a natural response, but you won't have it forever. Don't beat yourself up. You're the strongest person I know."

"You're a huge, beastly pro football player. You know people who could bench press me with one hand."

"And I can tell you with certainty they'd crumble under the reality that you lived through. Trust me, you're the strongest person I know, and I'm fucking honored that you're mine."

The last of her insecurity seems to fade, and she offers

me that small smile I love so much. "Thank you, Gabe. For always just letting me be me, insecure moments and all."

I grab her hand and kiss the back, keeping our fingers laced together. I rest our hands on my thigh for the remainder of the drive home and let out a sigh of contentment.

Queen of my heart and the love of my life, even if I haven't confessed that to her yet.

## THIRTY-ONE

# Danae

My gaze flickers between the Spanish subtitles and the image on the TV as the characters fight. As much as I love reading, I've never been a big fan of subtitles on movies. I prefer to be able to watch the screen and get drawn into the story via the image, *or* read the words on a page, but never both at the same time. But Gabe's mom texted me about getting together next week, and his sisters and I have been texting ever since his cousin's quince. In one of those texts, Cami mentioned how much their mom is obsessed with telenovelas, and honestly, I can see why. I've been watching them every spare chance I get, even though I'm pretty sure some of the subtitle translations aren't quite right. There was one about a duck that didn't make any sense in the context of the situation.

A throat clears, and I pause the TV and turn around to see Gabe standing behind me, a knowing smirk on his face.

"What are you watching?"

"Um, it's a telenovela Cami recommended."

His eyes light up, but there's also a slight twitch to his

eyebrow as if he doesn't really understand what I'm doing. "Why?"

"I heard it's your mom's favorite, and I really want her to like me, so I thought maybe if I watched some episodes it would give us something to talk about when she comes over next week."

He sits down next to me and drapes his arm over the back of the couch behind my head. "She already likes you. You don't have to do anything but just be yourself." He watches with me for a few minutes before he frowns at the screen. "That translation isn't right. Do you understand what's going on?"

"I think so. There's one woman and two brothers."

"Yeah, and she's in love with both of them."

"Wait, I thought she was just friends with that one," I say, pointing to the man who's currently on the screen, but Gabe is already shaking his head. "She is, but she's been in love with him for years. His brother has been in love with her, so he pursues her and she thinks that if she hooks up with that brother, the brother she's really in love with will finally see her as more than a friend. And spoiler, it works, but what she didn't expect was to fall in love with the other brother. Oh, and also they're stepbrothers, not blood brothers."

I know some of the translation was wrong, but he knows way more backstory than he should. "You've watched this one before."

He smiles wide, that same mischievous smile that I fall in love with more every day. "Only once or twice. My mom always had these shows playing in the background whenever I was home. I've learned some very cheesy Spanish one-liners that I hate to admit I used to pick up girls in college. They had no idea what I was saying, but it sounded good to them."

I laugh, a full body, hearty laugh, and when I finally catch my breath and turn to him, his entire face is lit up with happiness. "There's no better sound in the world than your laugh. And that's saying a lot because hearing you scream my name while I make you come is up there too."

My cheeks heat, but my heart feels like it's expanding bigger in my chest with every inhale. I've never felt like this before, and I know it's all due to the man sitting next to me.

Leaning my head on his shoulder, I turn back to the show, but don't really pay attention. "My mom used to watch soap operas, and whenever I was home sick, we'd snuggle on the couch together and watch them."

"You don't talk about her that often," he murmurs, his breath fanning against my head before he drops a kiss to my hair.

"There are a lot of good memories, but sometimes it's hard to think about the happy memories when you're buried so far beneath the reality of life. I don't know; it's hard to explain. Some days those memories kept me from giving up and others, they made giving up look so easy, especially when it had been so, so long since I'd experienced anything happy." I tilt my head to meet his gaze. "Until you. You've made me really happy, Gabe."

He leans forward and kisses me. It's different from all of our previous kisses—there's an emotion behind it that's gone unspoken but fills every gaping wound I've ever carried inside of me. His lips mold over mine as his tongue glides along my lips until they part and he slides along my tongue. There's heat, but it's like a low simmer that you feel in every inch of your body, warming you up slowly but so perfectly you don't ever want to stop.

When he pulls away, the emotion I felt in his kiss shines clear as day in his eyes, making my heart stutter. "My goal for the rest of my life is to make you as happy as possible, just so you know." He keeps his voice low, but the impact of his words reverberates through me as if he'd used a megaphone.

I let out a soft sigh and then lean back against him, my body truly relaxed for the first time in a long time.

I never want to lose this feeling.

A week later, Gabe's mom upholds her promise to come over and teach me how to make tamales while Gabe is at practice. But when she shows up, she's not alone. Both of Gabe's sisters, Cami and Ella, are with her, and each of them is carrying large reusable shopping bags overflowing with ingredients.

"I hope you don't mind, but I thought this might be more fun if we turned it into a *tamalada*," Nina says with a radiant smile. She walks into the house with confidence that suggests she comes over often, although this is only the second time I've seen her here in the two-plus months I've been here.

"What's a tamalada?" I whisper to Cami as she passes.

"It's a tamal making party. And trust me," she says conspiratorially, "it's much better than one-on-one because tamales can take *forever*."

Nina's smile is easy. "Everyone brings something and then we assemble them together. It cuts down on the workload significantly, and everyone leaves with more than enough tamales. Gabe used to always eat three or four before I even put them away."

I laugh at the picture of a young Gabe stuffing his face with tamales.

"Mom's been prepping the ingredients for days, so it should only take a couple of hours, especially with the four of us to cut down on assembling time. We'll have dozens ready in no time," Ella adds.

They move into the kitchen following their mother, and after I close the front door and take a deep, steadying inhale, I follow.

The kitchen is chaos as the three women bark out directions to each other in that way that only family can—both demanding and affectionate. They speak in a mix of Spanish and English, so I'm only half following what's going on as they all seem to decide on roles. Nina puts lard into the kitchen stand mixer that I've never seen Gabe use and gets to work on preparing the masa. Ella fills a huge pot with water and then rinses the corn husks before putting them in the pot. Then she takes a heavy-looking stone bowl and sets it on top of the corn husks. "This is a molcajete," she explains. "We use it to hold down the corn husks while they soak." She moves the pot to the side and sets a timer for an hour.

"Once the timer goes off, we'll check to make sure they're soft enough. If they are, then we'll pat them dry with paper towels and they'll be ready for fillings. Don't worry, I'll walk you through it."

"Okay," I say, already completely overwhelmed.

Cami walks over and pats my arm on her way to the fridge. "It's a lot. Now just imagine if we were actually cooking everything today instead of just warming up some things and making the masa."

"What can I help with?"

Nina turns to me with the most serious expression I've ever seen on her face. "How are you at mixing drinks?"

I fight back a smirk, but fail miserably. "I worked at a bar once. I'm pretty good."

She smiles and nods. "Good, then you can help Ella make us some drinks."

We work on our own individual tasks, prepping all the ingredients and waiting for the corn husks to be ready. Our conversation flows easily, and I'm grateful to Cami and Ella for carrying so much of the discussion. I half expected this to be an interrogation, but it's not.

If anything, with every moment that passes, they make me feel more like family.

Once everything is ready, we move to the table and lay everything out. Nina teaches me how to make a tamale, laying the corn husk flat with the narrow part facing away from me. Cami, who's sitting next to me, helps me when I put my masa too close to the right edge instead of leaving room like I notice they all have. Then I add my chosen fillings. Nina has outdone herself with a selection of chorizo, pork in red chili sauce, chicken in a salsa verde, and jalapeños with a Mexican cheese that balances the spice of the pepper.

Once I've successfully wrapped my tamales—we're not mentioning the first one that nearly fell apart as soon as I picked it up—Nina takes them over to the steamer she's set up on the stove. Then she comes back carrying the pitcher of the tequila sunrise I made during our earlier prep.

She tops off our drinks and then sits down, lifting her glass in a toast. "To familia, new and old," she says with a wink to me. I smile into my glass as I take a sip and warmth tingles down my spine. It could be the tequila, but deep in my bones, I know it's the acceptance of Gabe's family.

Getting started assembling the next round of tamales that will go in the steamer once the current ones are done, Nina asks, "So Danae, where's your family live?"

Her tone is casual and innocuous. She doesn't know my family is a touchy subject for me. "Um, well." I take another large gulp of my drink and then say, "I never knew my dad."

She hums a quiet acknowledgment of my words, and when I glance up at her she's watching me carefully. "And your mom, mija?"

I've been around Gabe long enough to pick up on some Spanish terms, though the only one he uses regularly is mi reina. I'm pretty sure *mija* is short for mi hija—my daughter.

I attempt to swallow the knot of emotion building in my throat, but the same pain that always rises when I talk about my mom swirls to life in my belly. "She passed away when I was eighteen. A car accident."

Nina looks stricken, and Cami reaches out to place her hand over mine. When I look over at her, her eyes are filled with compassion. Ella's as well.

"*Pobrecita*," Nina says, her hand going over her heart and her eyes filling with tears that don't spill. "I'm so sorry."

"It is what it is," I say with a shrug that's too practiced. "I've accepted it. It's just been a long time since I've done something like this." I gesture toward the table and the women surrounding me.

"This?" Ella asks.

It's a lot harder to swallow my emotions down this time, and my voice chokes when I speak. "Felt like part of a family."

A weighted solemnness descends on the table, and I'm mad at myself for putting a damper on the fun day we've all been having.

A hand rests on my wrist, and I look up into Nina's kind, loving eyes. "You are a part of our family, mija." Her voice is soft, but filled with conviction.

"Thank you, Nina," I whisper, not because I want to be quiet but because I'm trying so hard not to cry.

She nods as if she understands what I don't say—thank you for accepting me into your family, thank you for making me a part of this family tradition, thank you for raising a man who finally gave me hope in love, thank you for so much more than I could ever voice.

"You don't have to thank me," she says. "I should be thanking you. You've come into my son's life and made him happier than I've ever seen him. I thought he'd end up marrying a football because it seemed to be the only thing that gave him joy. But now he has you."

Yes, he does. He has me more than he probably knows.

"And don't worry, you'll be sick of us in no time," Cami says, lifting the conversation. "Now that you know how to make tamales, we'll rope you into making buñelos, menudo, and helping out with the next quince. I hope you're ready." She winks, and then Ella changes the conversation to a movie they both saw—Cami on a horrible first date and Ella with her best friend. I add to the conversation when I can, but I spend most of the next hour thinking about all the things they don't know about me.

Would they still be thankful that I've made Gabe happy if they knew that my very presence is also putting him in danger?

Would they think less of me if they knew I stayed with an abusive man for months, taking his abuse and believing the lies when he said it wouldn't happen again, only for it to happen more and more often?

Would they look at me with pity the same way my elderly neighbor, Mrs. Crawford, did when she realized what had been going on?

Can a woman with my history really get a happily ever after, or am I living my fairy tale on borrowed time?

# THIRTY-TWO

# Gabe

The ref's whistle pierces through the screams and cheers of the crowd, and I run toward the sideline as our offense takes the field. A quick glance at the scoreboard makes my pulse race. This game determines whether or not we go to the NFC Championship, and the score is closer than I'd like. Someone hands me a water bottle and I spray some into my mouth and then all over my face, quickly shaking it off. Ty comes up to me and stands with his back to the bench where Dom is sitting.

I'm kind of pissed at him right now. They scored a touchdown because he's letting his personal shit fuck with his head.

Turns out the truth of where he went on his birthday blew up in spectacular fashion when he was found naked outside of the townhouse of a very famous, very *married* celebrity. Dom's done a lot of fucked-up shit, but this one has had a domino effect that is now impacting the team. The entire coaching staff is pissed, and I'm pretty sure Coach Fairbright would've benched him completely if we didn't need him so badly.

The thin ice he was already on just thawed big-time.

"I know you're pissed at him," Ty mumbles next to me.

"He's playing like shit. We've got to be tight to keep these assholes from getting through any gaps. They shouldn't have gotten that touchdown."

Ever the peacemaker, he says, "I know, but dude, he's already getting hit below the belt repeatedly. First with Fairbright riding his ass, then the rumor that Denton wants to trade him because of all his antics, and now Alayna."

I twist my head to face him. "What about her?"

He shakes his head. "I don't know all the details. Dom was kind of a mess, but it sounds like she's pulled the plug on their friendship. Can't say I blame her. He bailed on her and left her to clean up and deal with his birthday party while he fucked a celebrity."

My scowl thickens. "Don't remind me."

"Listen. What I'm trying to say is that he needs us. We're his brothers, and right now, we might be all he's got. If you want him to play the way we all know he can, then he needs to know we've got his back out there. Go talk to him."

I glance back at him just in time to see Romel stand and pat him on the back before walking over to us.

"Did Ty convince you to talk to him too?" I ask.

"Nah, I just didn't feel like beating a dog when he was down."

"So I'm the hard-ass of the group now?"

Both Ty and Romel look at me and shrug. Fuck. I don't want to be a hard-ass. I don't even know why I'm so mad about this. Maybe because I can practically taste the Super Bowl. Maybe because he's making us look like shit out there, and I've got Danae standing with the other wives and girlfriends in the first row behind us and wanted her to see us at our best.

Whatever it is, Ty's right. Dom's our brother, and I need to pull my head out of my ass and show him we've all got his back, no matter what happens. Without another word, I walk over to the bench and sit down heavily next to Dom, who's staring at his tablet with more focus than I've ever seen from him.

"Are you okay?" I wince because that's obviously the fucking dumbest question I could've asked. Of course, he's not okay.

"I'm sorry I've been playing like shit." He sets the tablet down and rubs his hand over his short hair, resting back along the bench. Any press recording the sidelines would see two players talking, faces serious and gazes locked on the field watching things play out. There'd be no notice of the waver in Dom's voice.

"I really fucked up this time," he says, and the defeat in his voice permeates the air.

I agree with him, but that's probably not the most supportive thing to say right now. "You can't be the first guy to get caught naked with a married celeb."

He grips his thigh on the side. "She swore they were separated, but I couldn't care less about her."

"You're talking about Alayna."

His faux composure cracks. "Yeah."

"You guys have been friends for a long time. She's dealt with your bullshit before. Maybe she just needs a little cooldown time."

He shakes his head. "Not this time. She was pretty clear she was done."

Jack runs a play that gets us fifteen yards from the end zone, and I know I'm running out of time.

"She's going to be even more pissed if she finds out you played like a pussy because she got in your head. She might be cursing your name, but we both know she's a die-hard Wolves fan and wants to see us go to the Super Bowl."

He turns his head to stare at me. "So what you're saying is I need to pull my shit together?"

"Pretty much."

He huffs out a laugh. "Are we straight?"

I slap his back. "Yeah, man. We're good." I hold up a fist waiting for him to pound it. "Brothers forever."

"Brothers forever," he says.

And then I stand, rub his hair, and push his head down.

"What the fuck, dude?"

"That's for telling Alayna about Taylor Swift."

He falls back against the bench, his hand over his chest, and a hearty laugh escapes him. That's what I want to see. Dom plays best when he can laugh off the bullshit.

He's not quite back to his usual self as we head into the fourth quarter, and when the clock finally ticks down to zero, we're only ahead by a field goal.

But those three points are all it takes to send us one step closer to the Super Bowl.

We go crazy, our fans go crazy, the whole stadium goes crazy. All our people rush the sidelines, and I don't even hesitate to open my arms when Danae launches herself at me. Her legs automatically wrap around my waist at the same time I grab her ass in a tight hold. I catch a glimpse of her bright eyes and slightly rosy cheeks from the cold before our lips are joined.

I couldn't tell you who started the kiss, but I have no intention of stopping it. I groan into her mouth and lick at the seam of her lips, which she parts with a gasp, and our tongues slide together in a kiss so deep, I swear I feel it in my toes.

She finally pulls away with a laugh. "You're going to the NFC Championship!"

My smile matches hers. "I thought you didn't care about football."

"Are you crazy?! If you care about it, I care about it. You guys were amazing out there."

Her excitement and newfound fandom is adorable, but what's even better is that she's wearing my jersey over her sweatshirt.

When I set her down and get the full visual—tight jeans that hug every perfect curve, and an LA Wolves jersey with my name and number on the back—I let out a groan.

"Reina, we need to go home right now."

"Why?" she asks, but there's a mischievous light in her eyes that tells me she knows exactly why.

I shake my head and make my excuses to the press to get to the locker room. It feels like it takes an eternity to get out of there, but when I finally lay my eyes on Danae again, that urgency to get her in our bed as soon as possible returns with full force.

When we get home, my suspicions that she knew exactly what she was doing are officially confirmed. I come out of the bathroom to find Danae on her knees on the bed wearing my jersey, and *only* my jersey.

I let out a growl and then race toward the bed, eliciting a squeal from her when I tackle her, holding back most of my weight so we tumble onto the bed instead of hitting it too hard and accidentally crushing her. She closes her eyes and laughs hard while she twists away from my tickling fingers. When I finally stop, she's panting and so fucking beautiful it hurts to breathe.

"I love you, mi reina."

Her smile softens, and her eyes fill with a warmth I will

never tire of seeing. Her hand reaches up to cup my cheek. "I love you too, mi rey."

I inhale sharply at her words. She's always called me Gabe, which never bothered me, but this—calling me a term of endearment that mirrors the one I use for her—means more than I have words for.

So I don't use words.

I use my hands, my lips, my tongue. I make love to her with every piece of me, bringing her up to the crest multiple times before I let her tip over. Her legs shake around my neck as her thighs squeeze the sides of my head and I taste her release on my tongue. Her fingers pull my hair so tightly, I wonder if she's actually pulling some of it out. It'd be worth it. Her taste is divine.

When I finally slide inside her, we both let out groans of bliss. Our bodies move with practiced ease, knowing exactly how to touch each other to maximize our pleasure.

Roaming hands.

Panting breaths.

Rocking bodies.

We kiss deeper as our climax peaks and takes us over together, leaving me more spent than I've ever been in my life. I pull her close to my sweaty, naked body, and kiss the top of her head as her arm rests on my waist, her head in the crook of my shoulder, and sleep pulls me under with one final thought.

Life doesn't get any better than this.

# THIRTY-THREE

# Danae

A yawn cracks my jaw and I stretch my arms overhead, my body deliciously sore from the multiple celebratory rounds of sex last night. We both fell asleep after the first round, but sometime in the middle of the night, Gabe woke me up with his head between my legs, and that was like the starting gun for some seriously acrobatic sex.

Gabe is still passed out next to me, lying on his stomach, his face lax with sleep and one arm curled over his head. He looks younger when he's asleep, but no less strong.

A blissfully happy sigh escapes me as my gaze traces over his eyebrows, nose, lips. I feel like Gabe is my reward for surviving all the shit I've had to deal with in my life, and I've never been so thankful that I didn't give up.

Rolling over, I reach for my phone. I promised Cami I'd text her about getting together for lunch today. Except I never get a chance to text her because as soon as I turn on my phone, I'm bombarded by notifications.

At the tamalada, Ella taught me how to put on Google alerts so I could be kept up to date with any news about

Gabe or the LA Wolves. I just never thought that news would include me.

*Who's Gabe Romero's new lady love?*

*NFL hottie, Gabe Romero, off the market?*

*Fierce Four powerhouse kisses girlfriend after big win.*

My stomach drops as article after article pops up and then I see a video that must've been taken by one of the press on the sidelines. Funny, I've been so careful all this time, but I didn't even think about the fact that Gabe's game was being broadcast nationally. All I cared about was watching the man I'm in love with be successful at the game he loves.

None of my usual instincts had kicked in when I rushed onto the field and jumped straight into his arms. All I felt was euphoria—like *I'd* just been the one to win the game and not him. I didn't think about the cameras on the sidelines or the press doing interviews with other players still on the field.

Why didn't I think about that? Why didn't I consider that by kissing him in the middle of everyone, *my* face would suddenly be the one everyone talked about?

I didn't think my stomach could sink any further but it does. My face is plastered all over the Internet. Mitch has found me with a whole lot less than that. There's no way he'll miss this. He's going to know where I am, who I'm with.

"Oh my God."

I don't even realize I've said the words out loud until I feel Gabe move behind me, dropping a kiss to my shoulder. Groggily, he asks, "What is it?"

My voice sounds hollow when I answer. "They took pictures of us on the field."

He glances over my shoulder where I hold my phone in

my hand and looks at the screen. A smile lights his face before he kisses my shoulder again and panic starts to seize me. "Damn, reina. You look good wrapped around me like that. We should frame this one."

I know he just woke up, so I'll give him the benefit of the doubt that he's not being insensitive on purpose. He's not used to living in fear or worrying about being found by a psycho ex.

"Gabe," I say, trying—and failing—to keep my tone even, but my panic slips through and his smile drops as his eyes furrow with concern. "He's going to see this," I whisper.

Realization dawns on his face, and his eyes dart between me and the screen of my phone before he lies back down and covers his face with his hands.

"Shit," he murmurs. "I'm so sorry. I didn't even think about that."

I've already been in LA longer than other places without him finding me. I knew it was only a matter of time, but this has made it an inevitability. The question now is how soon he'll show up here. How soon until he finds out where Gabe lives and ruins the first slice of happiness I've had in as long as I can remember.

Gabe sits up and pulls me into his arms, holding me tight against his body. "He won't get to you. You're safe with me."

But I know that's not true, and based on the frantic pace of Gabe's heart, I suspect he doesn't even believe his own words.

Mitch will find me. Just like he always does.

The next several days go by uneventfully. I run my usual errands, but Gabe makes sure there's always someone with me. I don't know if he's worried Mitch might abduct me, but I don't mind the company. Unfortunately, having one of his sisters or one of the other Wolves' ladies with me doesn't stop that niggling feeling that makes the hairs on the back of my neck stand on end. The feeling like I'm being watched. It's been a long time since I've felt it, and I can't tell if it's paranoia or if my gut is warning me of a danger I can't see.

By the third day, I decide not to bother running errands. I'm tired of coming home frazzled and exhausted from being emotionally on edge the whole time. I spend the day hiding in the library, escaping into other worlds and pausing periodically to work on a project of my own.

I've just stepped into the kitchen for a lunch break when I hear the doorbell ring. Assuming it's a package delivery because no one's expected to drop by, I take my time heading to the door. When I open it, no one's there and no cars are out front. The street is quiet. But on the doorstep is a small postcard with *Greetings from Boston* printed on the front in bright orange with cartoon drawings of some of the most popular tourist destinations. When I flip it over, I feel all the color drain from my face. Only two words are there, but they're enough to send me into a tailspin of panic.

*Miss me?*

My body moves before I'm even aware of what I'm doing, but I don't slow down as I race through the house, up the stairs two at a time, and straight into Gabe's room. I run to the closet where my clothes have made their way across from his. More garments than I've had in years line my side of the closet because he wanted me to be comfortable, to have whatever I wanted or needed. My frantic gaze darts around looking for a suitcase or bag or anything to stuff as much as I can into it.

I have to get out of here.

Finding one above his row of suits, I grab it and throw it onto the ground, my hands reaching around me and grabbing clothes in a mindless frenzy. I don't even realize I'm crying until my vision is so blurred, I can't see anything in front of me.

My knees give out and I collapse into a pile on the floor, tears streaming from my eyes and a keening wail ripping from my throat that doesn't even sound like me. This time is so much worse than every other time he's found me, and my heart is breaking at the thought of leaving Gabe.

I know I will do what's best to keep him safe, but God, I feel like someone's ripping my heart out with a dull set of kitchen knives.

Pushing myself up on shaky legs, I grab my haphazardly packed bag and head to the bathroom. I throw in as many toiletries as I can, all the while kicking myself for not having a bug-out bag ready. I knew this day was coming.

I always knew he'd find me.

But I didn't want him to.

I want Gabe.

His handsome face flashes in my mind, and I nearly stumble as I make my way toward my library, my heart shredding with every weighted step. Going inside only makes the pain hurt worse, but I refuse to leave without a book—something to always remember Gabe by, to remember what it felt like to be loved.

I suck in a shallow gasp that quickly turns into a heavy sob as I steady myself against the bookshelves.

Why did I ever have to meet Mitch? That sonofabitch has ruined everything in my life since the moment he came into it.

As I scan the hundreds of books Gabe bought for me, I realize that maybe if Mitch had never been in my life, Gabe might not have either. Would I ever have come to LA if I hadn't been on the run? Would I have been working in that bar? Would our paths have crossed or would we forever remain as strangers?

I hate Mitch for a lot of things, but I'll never hate him for driving me right into the arms of the love of my life.

I grab two books—an old favorite and a new one that Gabe had signed by the author—and then with one final glance, I leave the most thoughtful gift I've ever been given.

My legs are wobbly as I make my way down the stairs, my heart still racing and my hands shaking with a tremor I can't seem to stop no matter how much I try.

I step off the last stair and finally lift my gaze only for it to smack into Gabe, his keys still in his hands and the garage door open behind him. His brows are furrowed with concern as his eyes dart between me and the bag in my hand.

"What's going on?"

THIRTY-FOUR

# Gabe

My heart pounds as my brain tries to make sense of what I'm seeing—Danae standing at the bottom of the stairs, a packed bag held in a white-knuckled grip, her face red and splotchy, tears still streaking down her cheeks.

"What's going on?" I'm trying not to let my panic show, but she looks more spooked than I've ever seen her.

Her chest heaves, and I can't tell if she's going to burst into tears or throw up. She shakes her head and then crumples to the stairs as if her legs aren't strong enough to hold her up.

"I don't want to run anymore," she cries.

Her words should calm me, but they don't. It's an admittance of what I already suspected—she was going to leave me without so much as a goodbye.

Squatting down, I hold her face in my hands, brushing her tears away with my thumbs. "Mi reina," I whisper, my heart in my throat. "What the hell is going on?"

"He found me," she whispers, utter heartbreak and a healthy mix of fear and panic in her eyes. My panic shifts, now having something to focus on—a purpose.

"How do you know?"

She glances behind me, her eyes searching for something, and then finally she points at a spot on the floor to the side of the front door where an orange postcard lies. I place a kiss on her forehead and then move over to it, bending down to pick up the innocent looking piece of cardstock. When I flip it over, a chill tingles down my spine at the two innocent words printed in a tidy scrawl.

Flipping the card back over, I take notice of the *Greetings from Boston* printed on the front and remember that's where Danae was when Mitch found her last and she hopped on the first plane she could get, landing her here in LA. Turning the card in my hands, I see the subtle threat, the way he's taunting her, threatening her without actually saying anything threatening. His mere presence—the acknowledgment that he knows where she is—is enough.

Moving back to her, I pull her into my arms and carry her into the living room. Her sobs have turned into hiccups, and there's a slight tremor in her body as if she was out in the cold for too long and can't get warm. I've seen Danae exhausted, borderline hopeless, defensive, and skeptical. I've never seen her scared. It's sobering to see someone who I know as so strong completely fall apart.

It makes me wonder if Mitch is worse than she let on—if he did more than she admitted to me.

"He's not going to get to you," I murmur into her hair.

She tilts her head back, looking up at me with big eyes that look so forlorn. "He's already found me, Gabe," her voice breaks and I pull her against my chest.

"I can't lose you. I won't survive it. Te amo, mi reina. You're it for me." I cup her head and pull her back so she's forced to look in my eyes and see the determination in my gaze. "I will protect you, and if I can't, I'll hire someone to do it. We'll get all new security for the house and get you a bodyguard."

She shakes her head. "Gabe, no. I can't ask that of you."

"You're not. Don't you get it? If you leave me, I'll be a fucking shell without you. You're my heart, my queen, my whole soul. I never thought I'd feel this way about someone, but the only way I'm letting you walk out that door is if you tell me you're leaving because you don't love me, not because you're scared."

I hold her gaze until it drops to my chest. "That's what I thought," I mutter. "No more running, Danae. You're not alone anymore; we fight this bogeyman together."

"I don't want to run anymore. I don't want to leave you, but I'm so scared if I stay, he'll hurt you."

"I'll be okay. I'm more worried about you right now. Let's try added security and a bodyguard for a while and see how that goes, okay?"

She nods and then rests against me until all her adrenaline fades and she falls asleep. I gently place her on the couch and then go make phone calls.

Our new security company shows up a few days later. Rafferty Carmichael greets me with a firm handshake as he enters my house, his gaze scanning all the entrances and exits with a quick sweep. He's the co-owner of Carmichael Security, which came recommended from Cami's boss. They're a highly reputable company that does most of the security for high profile celebs. Apparently Cami's boss is best friends with Rafferty and put in a good word on my behalf. I doubt the owner usually does these initial setup meetings. He's joined by Wyatt Jones, one of his employees, and the primary bodyguard he's assigning to Danae.

"Thanks for coming so quickly," I say.

"When my best friend calls me and tells me I need to do

a favor for his assistant so she doesn't quit on him, I can't really say no, can I? That man would be insufferable if Cami didn't keep him in line. No thanks."

I laugh. "If only I knew who he was, but she's pretty mum about him."

He side-eyes me like he's not sure I'm telling the truth about not knowing the name of her boss. "Yeah, those pesky NDAs can be a bitch, can't they? Anyway, I'd like to take a walk-through. Wyatt and I will take notes on anything that needs to be changed or upgraded for optimum security and then we'll discuss her protection when she's out of the house."

"Sure thing," I say and gesture for him to go wherever he wants. Wyatt makes notes on his phone while they both walk around my property and point out blind spots that might be problematic and where they want to place security cameras.

Danae comes down the stairs right as we step back in the house, but stills when she sees the other guys with me. I hate how on edge she's been since I got home and found her packed and ready to run, but I'm determined to do whatever it takes to put her at ease.

"Danae, this is Rafferty and Wyatt, the guys from Carmichael Security."

She gives a wave and a weak smile that doesn't reach her eyes.

Rafferty steps forward, extending his hand and adjusting his posture to be less threatening. "You can call me Raff." When she shakes his hand, my own shoulders relax a little. "I'm sorry you're going through this, but we're going to do everything in our power to make sure this guy can't get to you."

"Thank you," she says, her voice soft and weak, and so unlike the strong, passionate woman I know her to be.

"Gabe said there was a postcard. Can we see it?"

She nods and moves over to the side table by the front door that has a small drawer typically used to hold junk I'll no doubt forget is there until I deep clean. On top of the few items in there rests the innocent looking postcard that is anything but innocent.

Raff flips it over in a similar fashion to how I did, his gaze taking in every single aspect of it. "Can you walk me through how you found it?"

She explains, her voice shaking when she describes finding the postcard. Her hands twist in her lap, and there's a subtle tremor in her body that not even my presence next to her can settle. I've heard this story twice now, and each time it sends a panicked chill down my spine. We can't be sure whether he delivered it himself or had someone else do it, but the idea that he was physically here makes my fists clench. He was so close to her. If he'd stayed at the door, he could've gotten to her as soon as she opened it. He could have grabbed her and kidnapped her, he could have come inside and hurt her—or worse. I fight against the nausea that hits me like a punch to the gut.

"Have you noticed anything suspicious around the house or neighborhood when you've gone out?" he asks her.

She shakes her head. "No. Everything has seemed normal." She hesitates and then looks at me with trepidation. "Except..."

Raff's eyes narrow as he watches her body language. "What is it?"

"A day or two after the media posted our picture, I thought I felt..."

Wyatt stands at attention, his gaze fixed on her, while

Raff sits at the edge of his seat, his body taut as he tries to ascertain any clue about what she might reveal.

"It felt like I was being watched." Her voice is a weak murmur. "It's the same feeling I've gotten every time he's found me."

"He's done this before?"

She lets out an unamused huff of laughter. "He's done this every one to three months for over a year and a half."

Raff doesn't give away what he thinks of this. "How's he finding you?"

She shakes her head. "I don't know. I've always used prepaid phones that I bought in the store, I use cash and fake names, get jobs working under the table, stay at cheap or innocuous places. I don't know how he keeps finding me, but he does. The last time..." Her voice cuts off with a choke, and when she's pulled herself together, she tells him about how he found her in Boston and her suspicions that he was behind her cousin's death.

Raff and Wyatt share a look and then Wyatt pulls out his phone and types something on it.

Raff focuses back on Danae. "We'll look into that. Until we get all the security stuff set up, I'm going to insist that Wyatt goes with you whenever you leave the house. Our guys can work quickly, but it'll take a couple of days to get everything exactly how I want it and all the cameras up."

"Okay," she says.

"The Championship game is tomorrow. Is it okay for her to be there?" I ask.

"That shouldn't be a problem," Raff says. "Switching up your routine might be a good thing. It's much harder to hit a moving target, and since you'll have a detail with you at all times, you'll be safe to move freely. Are you planning for her to sit in a box or near the field?"

"A box with a bunch of the other wives and girlfriends."

He glances over at Wyatt who nods. "I'll call the stadium and have Jaime do a security sweep before the game."

Raff nods before turning back to Danae. "I'm going to assign Jaime Walsh as Wyatt's relief, but Wyatt will be your primary protection, and Jaime will assist as necessary."

"You're sure it'll be safe for her to be there?" I ask.

Raff's response shows his patience and professionalism. I can't imagine I'm the first guy to be worried about the safety of his loved one. "She'll be safe with us, Gabe. You have my word." Raff pushes himself up to standing. "I need to head back to the office and get things scheduled for the security camera install. Wyatt's going to stay behind, and Jaime will be here to take the overnight shift."

Raff heads out and then Wyatt goes over the plan for the game tomorrow. He's confident and focused which puts me somewhat at ease, but the looming threat to Danae still causes a ball of anxiety to form in my gut.

As Wyatt does a lap around the perimeter of the house, I pull Danae into the safety of my arms—both for her benefit and for mine.

"How you holding up?" I ask her.

"I don't know." She pulls back enough to look me in the eyes. "I'm still scared, Gabe. I'll never forgive myself if you get hurt because of me."

"He's not going to hurt anyone, okay. He's never going to hurt you again." I try to put as much certainty behind my words as I can muster, but there's a part of me that's terrified no matter what I do, he'll get to her.

She hugs me tighter, burying her head in my chest. "I love you, Gabe. I'm sorry I almost ran."

"It's okay," I say, dropping a kiss to her head. I know it

was a reflex. It's all she's known for the past two years, but we're in this together now. She no longer has to fight this battle alone.

As Wyatt comes back in the house, some relief settles in my bones, but there's still a nagging feeling that I can't let my guard down. Not until Mitch is found.

# THIRTY-FIVE

# Danae

I hate feeling like a burden, and nothing enhances that like having your bodyguard clear the entire women's bathroom before you can use it.

Fortunately, it's a smaller bathroom on the VIP level of the stadium and not one of the general bathrooms that always have a line a mile long. I can only imagine the glares I would get then.

But what's even more ridiculous is the amount of cameras trying to get pictures of me. My phone has been blowing up with Google alerts and all of them are press images of our booth, me sitting front and center talking to Nikki, who's sitting next to me. I've already showed Wyatt, who informed me he's getting the alerts as well, but there's nothing we can do.

"All you need to do is enjoy the game. There's extra security presence here, so even though he knows your location, there's no way he can get to you. You're safe."

Easy for him to say. I don't feel safe. I feel like an animal in a cage, even though I'm free to go wherever I want as long as Wyatt's with me. And even worse, that niggling feeling that I'm being watched hasn't left me since we left the house. I'm on edge, my nerves frayed, because even if it's just press cameras and not Mitch watching me, it's still disconcerting. I've always lived under the radar—even when I was a nobody.

Now everyone is watching me, and it's only adding to my stress.

"Here," Nikki says as she passes me a small flask.

"What's this?" I ask as I take a healthy sip and then immediately sputter.

She laughs. "Easy. Pace yourself. That's top shelf whiskey. It's meant to be sipped, not guzzled."

"Interesting. I didn't see you as a whiskey girl," I say, my eyes watering and my throat a little scratchy. I take a second, much smaller sip and let the flavors burst on my tongue as a warmth spreads down my throat and my chest, settling in my stomach. "Okay, that's definitely much better in small doses."

"Told you," she says, taking the flask and putting it back in her bag.

"None for you?" I ask.

Dropping her voice, she says, "Oh no. I brought it for you. I knew this night was likely going to be stressful. Gabe gave me a rundown of what was going on when I ran into him in the office."

At my look of confusion, she clarifies. "I used to work for the Wolves, and my best friend, Cassie, still does, so I was there to see her for lunch and saw him talking to the head of security. I might've eavesdropped enough to follow him and ask him what was going on and what you needed."

I should probably be mad he told someone else about what's going on, but they were bound to find out anyway given my new shadow who's twice my size and could probably bench press me. He's hard to hide.

Clearing my throat, I say, "Oh, well, thank you."

She grabs my hand and looks me in the eyes. "We have to stick together. It's not easy loving a professional football player, but it's even harder when you've got your own shit going on. Then add the press to it and it's a disaster. No one understands that better than these women," she says gesturing around her. "We may not completely understand the fear you probably feel, but you're not alone. We've got your back, Danae. You're part of the group now."

I feel her words—I feel a part of a group of strong, resilient women. Squeezing her hand back, I say sincerely, "Thank you, Nikki."

Then she raises her voice and announces, "Let me know if you want more. I can't drink anyway...not for the foreseeable future at least." She winks at me, and I arch my brow, wondering if she's going where I think she's going when Paige spins in her seat to face Nikki with pure joy on her face.

"Nikki! Are you pregnant?"

Nikki smiles wide, her skin glowing so obviously I wonder how I missed it. "I am!"

The girls squeal in excitement, and before she gets wrapped up in a million hugs, she leans over and whispers to me, "Matt's announcing it after the game, which should take all the heat off you and Gabe. Nothing gets the press giddy like a baby out of wedlock," she adds with a roll of her eyes.

When she pulls all the way back, an understanding bounces between us, and I wonder if that announcement was planned or if they decided to move it forward to help me get a break from the press that's hounded my every move for the past week—and served as a giant red arrow for Mitch to know where I am at all times. Either way, I'm grateful all the same.

The women around me all share in the joy and excitement with Nikki, Paige sharing tricks she's learned so far during her pregnancy and discussing the future. The air around me lifts from weighted and tense to joyful and light. Maybe it's the whiskey, but my nerves seem slightly less frayed as we all enjoy ourselves and watch our men play.

It's only when I glance back at the sentry who stands by the door that my fear slithers back to the surface.

But Mitch has taken enough from me. I deserve to enjoy this night with my newfound friends and watch the love of my life play the game he's so good at. I can choose to enjoy the night or let the threat of what Mitch might do ruin it. Facing forward and looking out onto the field, I choose to enjoy it.

# THIRTY-SIX

# Gabe

From the first moment I picked up a football, I never had a problem focusing on the field in front of me—being one hundred percent committed to the game that was my first love. Unfortunately, the one night I need to be more focused than ever also happens to be the night I can't stop worrying about Danae's safety.

"What's going on with you?" Dom asks. "I thought I was supposed to be the fuckup of this group."

I shake him off, but he grabs my arm and pulls me back. "Dude, seriously. What the fuck?"

I glance up at the VIP box where I know Danae is with the other WAGs. I *know* she's safe. I *know* Wyatt is with her and I'm paying Carmichael Security a small fortune to keep her safe. But knowing doesn't change the unease that swirls like a disease in my gut.

Something's coming. Something bad. I haven't been able to shake the feeling all day that he's going to try to pull something here in the chaos of all these people.

A whistle blows and I brush him off. "Not now. We've got a game to play."

I walk away, but I can feel the weight of my teammate's stare on my back. I'm not the guy who loses his head, who has an attitude on or off the field. But apparently I'm that guy tonight.

We get on the field and into position. As a strong safety, I'm the last line of defense in the backfield—it's my job to stop the ball from coming into the end zone, and it's one I'm fucking good at. Fortunately, I've studied this team and these plays so well, my slight distraction won't stop me from continuing to be the best of the best.

Channeling all my frustrations into the douchebag coming toward me with the ball, I rush forward, easily switching directions when he tries to dodge me, and then tackling him to the ground ten yards from the end zone.

I jump up and am just about to turn around when I hear him say, "You ain't shit, Romero. Fuckin' pussy-ass bitch."

I spin around just as he stands and immediately shove him back. He rushes forward and our face guards clack as we get in each other's faces, shouting unintelligible obsceni-ties at each other. I'm about to shove him again when two sets of hands pull me back and then Romel's in my face, shoving me farther away from him. "What the fuck are you doing?"

Dom stands next to him, still holding onto my pads as if I'd rush back to that piece of shit from the other team. Both of them look at me like they don't know who I am.

I shove their hands off me. "Get off. I'm fine."

"The fuck you are," Romel says as Ty comes running over to us.

"What the fuck's going on?"

I gesture over to the other player who's now surrounded by a few of his own teammates. "That fucking piece of shit's got a big mouth."

"I'm gonna beat your ass, Romero!" I hear his shout and that causes me to push forward, but Romel, Dom, and Ty are already shoving me back while the refs come running over, blowing their whistles.

The guys are talking to me, but I can no longer hear them over the whooshing in my ears as my adrenaline starts to subside.

A ref comes jogging over. "Everything okay over here?"

"Yeah, he's good," Ty says, but it's not enough for the ref who looks me square in the eyes. "Romero?"

I clench my jaw and then nod. "Yeah. I'm good."

He nods once. "You do that again, and I'll throw a flag. Play a clean game, guys."

He jogs away and the players reset in order to resume play. I've never been the cause of delay—no matter how small—and shame joins the unease growing in my gut.

I've never hated anyone in my life, but right now I hate Mitch. I hate that he's threatening the love of my life. I hate that his mere existence is fucking with my head.

I manage to keep myself together for the remainder of the half, but just barely. Dom and Ty both have to pull me back when another guy, who seems to be buddy-buddy with the guy I shoved before, tries taunting me. Romel gives me his dad glare, which I'm sure gets his two-year-old in line, but doesn't exactly work on me when I know I could take him.

Taunting on the field is nothing new, and it's never been a problem for me before, but tonight is not the night to fuck with me. I'm too on edge and every single slight only sets me off.

When we head into the locker room during halftime, the guys pull me aside and shove me against the wall, their glowering faces piercing me as they surround me.

"You better start talking and tell us what the fuck is up with you because the shit you're pulling out there ain't cool, brother," Dom says, while Romel stands with his arms crossed. Ty's jaw is clenched as hard as his fists at his side.

Swallowing my pride, I tell them everything, or everything I can in a few minutes.

Romel's accusatory face has transitioned to sympathetic, but his words are cutting. "I feel for ya, man, but you have got to get your head together out there or Fairbright's gonna bench your ass."

"Actually, I'm benching his ass no matter what," a female voice says behind the guys and they spin, revealing our defensive coach, her hard gaze instantly finding mine. "Sorry, Gabe, but we can't risk it this close to the Super Bowl. I'm benching you and putting in Shaw. I've already filled in Denton."

My stomach heats with anger—at myself, at Mitch, at how out of my control everything feels—and I turn around and punch the wall. Pain immediately shoots through my hand, and regret hits me hard and heavy.

I drop my head to the wall. There's shuffling of cleats and then a door opens and closes and Fairbright moves to lean against the wall next to me. "I'm sorry, Gabe."

"It's not your fault," I mumble. It's true. This is entirely of my own making. I'm just fucking pissed at myself for doing it. I've let my team down. I've let myself down. I've probably even let Danae down.

I didn't think I could feel any worse about myself until that thought floats through my mind and I think about how it would've looked from her perspective. How she suffered at the hands of an abusive man and then watched me nearly get in two brawls on the field.

This night can't get any worse.

# THIRTY-SEVEN

# Danae

I spoke too soon.

Nikki's whiskey fix was so temporary, it didn't even last for a quarter. I've tried to ignore my anxiety ever since, but it's only halftime and I feel like I'm going crazy. My heart is racing and my eyes are constantly darting around at people in the crowd, wondering if Mitch is among them. I've barely been able to focus on anything happening on the field, even when the girls made a comment about how out of character Gabe was acting.

I feel like the worst girlfriend in the world because I didn't even notice him on the field among the bodies moving chaotically from this distance. I can't see anything through the black that dims my vision from my panic and refuses to fully recede.

Everyone is in high spirits, laughing and chatting comfortably around me as the players run back on the field. I roll my shoulders, hoping it might loosen them up a little, and feel a deep pain under the muscle from how long I've been clenching them.

Nikki leans forward, her gaze locked on the players. "Is Gabe injured?"

The chatter subsides as everyone focuses on the field. "I don't think so," Paige says, "but I don't see him on the field."

Nikki gestures to the sideline. "Because he's sitting on the bench."

The rest of the defense gets in position, and my vision focuses enough to see another player in the spot where Gabe normally stands.

"Weird. Maybe it's just temporary?" Paige says like a question.

"Maybe," Nikki mumbles with a glance to me, and I know we're thinking the same thing. Gabe's out of character behavior is because of me—for the same reason I've been riding the edge of a panic attack since we got here.

Knowing the burden I've brought into Gabe's life has now impacted how he plays the sport he loves tips me over the edge. The room tilts, and all I hear is my name being called from far away and then nothing.

When I come to, Wyatt is kneeling over me with a water bottle ready to go. His gaze is steady as he asks, "How you feeling?"

"Embarrassed," I murmur, sitting up as it hits me that I just panicked myself into a fainting spell.

"Nothin' to be embarrassed about." He leans forward conspiratorially. "I had a guy piss himself once."

"You did not," I say, but a smile tips my lips up and he smirks.

"Maybe I did, maybe I didn't. It'd be unprofessional to confirm or deny."

I chuckle and then take a sip of water. "Thanks," I whisper, feeling less embarrassed but still on edge.

Wyatt's eagle-eyed gaze narrows. "Is this too much?"

My heart sinks, and I nibble my lip while I fight back hot, angry tears. Instead of speaking, I nod.

"Alright. What do you want to do? Stay or go?"

Am I the worst girlfriend in the world if I leave before the game's over?

"You don't have to stay, Danae. Gabe would understand," Nikki says as she kneels down on my other side with a plate of snacks for me. "I texted a contact and they said word is Gabe is benched for the rest of the game. Coaches didn't want him to get a flag and cause a penalty."

Leaning forward, I drop my head into my hands. "This is all my fault."

"No, it's not," Nikki says, placing a delicate hand on my upper back. "It's okay to ask for what you need. If you need to go home, no one here is going to think any less of you."

"But I will," I say, looking up at her. "I'll think less of me because I wasn't strong enough to keep my shit together and support my boyfriend during one of the biggest games of his career."

"Technically, the Super Bowl will be the biggest game," Paige adds. "And they're going, or else Jack will be an insufferable grump for weeks. They all need a time-out once in a while. It's about time Gabe had his. Don't feel bad about that and don't take on his problems. Let him handle himself and you deal with your stuff. We can text you updates, but I know he'll understand."

He will. He's always been understanding and accepting of my needs, even when I wasn't. I just wish for once I could be here for him instead of dealing with my own shit.

"Okay," I say, accepting defeat. I look at Wyatt. "I need to go home."

He nods and helps me up. Once I'm on my feet, I grab my stuff and then he escorts me out of the VIP box into the hall where two security guards stand waiting. Wyatt barks out instructions for both of them and one leads the way to where he's parked the SUV, while the other follows behind Wyatt, who stands next to me, his body tense, but also somehow at the ready. I keep my head down as we walk past small clusters of people and then a sudden shout has my heart jumping. A quick glance back and it steadies when I see it's just a group of overactive teenagers—two boys trying to impress some girls.

The parking lot is empty, but there's always been something menacing about parking lots at night. There are too many places for him to hide, and my heart starts racing again while my palms get sweaty. My gaze darts around the lot, and even though I'm surrounded by security and have Wyatt at my side, I can't help feeling exposed.

Is Mitch here? Is he watching me from one of these cars, hidden in the shadows? A knot forms in my throat as panic settles into my bones. Wyatt opens the door to the back seat of the SUV and glances in the back as part of his protocol before ushering me inside. I'm buckled and gripping the door handle by the time he gets in the car and starts it.

It feels like it takes forever to get on the highway and head toward the safety of Gabe's house, but I know it's only maybe ten, fifteen minutes tops. It'll be another thirty minutes before we're back at the house, and I can finally relax.

We've just exited off the highway when a sharp pop sounds from the other side of the car, and Wyatt swerves slightly with a curse before pulling over to the side of the dark road.

"What's going on?" I say, my voice shaking as my gaze darts into the shadowy darkness outside the vehicle. Why aren't there more streetlights here?

"Hold on." Wyatt gazes out the window and then spins to me. "Stay put, okay? I'm gonna check it out."

I nod, my voice buried under my fear.

He gets out of the car and then reengages the locks. I watch him walk to the rear tire on the passenger side and squat down out of sight. When he stands back up, he looks around and pulls a small flashlight out of his suit pocket. He flashes it into the darkness, scanning the surroundings. I don't see anything, and he must not either because he comes back around to my side of the door and disengages the lock.

He opens my door. "It's a flat tire. Looks like we drove over some debris from an accident. I'm going to change it real quick and then we'll be on our way, okay?"

I glance behind him, my eyes flitting from side to side. "What if it's him?"

What if this was exactly what Mitch wanted? Get me away from the crowd? What if this isn't a coincidence at all? When it comes to Mitch, I wouldn't put anything past him.

Wyatt dips his head enough so we're eye level. "He's not here, and even if he was, he'd have to go through me to get to you, and that ain't happenin'."

"Okay," I say, my voice soft and weak.

But he doesn't know Mitch—the way his mind works, the head games he likes to play.

I do. And that niggling sensation in my gut won't let go of the feeling that this is just another way he's messing with me.

Wyatt closes the door and then moves to the back where he grabs the spare tire and a jack. He engages the locks and then gets to work. The minutes tick by, each one feeling longer than the last. My heart is more frantic than a rabbit being chased by a fox. The hairs on the back of my arms rise and my body goes on high alert. The sound of the locks disengaging rips a gasp from my mouth, and my head whips around only to find Wyatt opening up the back and putting the busted tire where the spare was. He stows the jack, closes the back door, and gets back in the driver's seat. He pulls the car onto the road as if nothing happened. As if I haven't been sitting here expecting to be murdered on the side of the road for the last ten minutes.

I drop my head into my hands and rest my elbows on my knees. "I feel like I'm losing my fucking mind," I whisper.

"What was that?" Wyatt asks.

"Nothing," I say louder and then lean back against the seat.

I'm sick of being taunted and of this mental warfare Mitch is playing. I don't want to play anymore. Not for the first time, I wish a restraining order wasn't just a piece of paper. I wish there were more laws in place to protect women from men like Mitch instead of forcing us to fend for ourselves. While I don't feel hopeless like I did the night Gabe and I met, I am exhausted—mentally, emotionally, physically.

We pull up to the house, and as soon as we walk through the front doors, all the stress of the past several hours fades away.

I'm home.

It's crazy how good it feels to have a home. After so long on the run, it almost felt like a far-fetched dream, but Gabe has made it a reality. He gave me a home and a place I feel safe. He taught me to trust again and showed me what real love looks like.

And it feels so freaking good. Even with all the bullshit with Mitch hanging over my head.

"Thank you for tonight, Wyatt. I'm sorry I was so worked up earlier."

He smiles. "No need to apologize. I get it. You staying in your room for the rest of the night?"

"I think so. I'm exhausted."

"Alright," he says with a nod. "Lead the way. I wanna do a sweep and then I'll get out of your hair and do a sweep of the rest of the house."

"Thanks, Wyatt."

"Just doing my job."

That may be true, but I do feel safer knowing he's here. "When do you and Jaime switch?"

"He'll be on in the morning to give me a break, but I'll be here throughout the night."

"Okay," I say, and then we head upstairs.

Wyatt does a thorough sweep of our room, including the closet, the bathroom, and even under the bed. Where was this man when I believed in monsters as a child?

"All clear. I'll be either downstairs or doing rounds if you need me." He sets a small device on my nightstand. "That's a panic button, just in case. Press it and I'll get an immediate alert, okay?"

"Okay," I say, already feeling more at ease with the button nearby. "Night," I say and then do my usual routine of getting ready for bed.

As exhausted as I am, as soon as my head hits the pillow, my mind is wide awake and no amount of lying there will shut it off enough for sleep to pull me under. Finally giving up, I kick the covers off and decide to get some tea. I'll grab it and bring it to my library and curl up with a book until my mind settles enough for me to finally fall asleep, or whenever Gabe comes home, whichever comes first.

I'm halfway to the door when I remember the panic

button and dart back to grab it, holding it in my hand since my sleep shorts don't have pockets. The hallway is dark and the house quiet as I make my way downstairs. I step off the stairs and glance around the unlit dining room and living room. I can see through the large glass doors and windows that Wyatt is right outside talking on his phone, facing the pool.

Moving into the kitchen, I put the panic button on the counter and then move around the kitchen getting a kettle of water boiling and pulling a chamomile tea bag and some honey from the cupboard. There's a shuffle of footsteps behind me and I turn around, expecting to find Wyatt back inside the house, but instead it's my worst nightmare come to life.

"Mitch." His name is a weak whisper that barely makes a sound. I glance to the side of the kitchen and realize my error in coming in here without alerting Wyatt. There's a wall that blocks the view of the backyard from where both Mitch and I are standing. My gaze darts to the panic button on the counter *behind* where Mitch stands menacingly with a knife in his gloved hand.

My eyes dart up to his and lock on the ice-cold blue depths that show no other feeling except for glee at the terror he's brought to life in me. I open my mouth to scream but he's faster, lunging forward. I flinch, expecting to be stabbed to death, but instead he wraps his body around mine and covers my mouth and nose tightly with his hand until black dots mar my vision.

"You thought you could run and hide from me forever? You're *mine*."

When my knees start to buckle from the lack of oxygen, he lowers his hand so it only covers my mouth, but his grip is strong and my jaw already aches from how tight he's holding me.

The cool metal of his blade glides across my cleavage and chest before sliding up to my neck. Tears burn hot as they streak down my face, and even though he's no longer covering my nose, it still feels impossible to breathe.

"I'll admit, you hid pretty well this time. No matter how hard my private investigators searched, they couldn't figure out where you'd gone." He rubs his nose along my cheek, inhaling and then humming as if pleased. "Then imagine my surprise when I'm watching a football recap and the broadcaster shows you wrapping your slutty self around the famous Gabe Romero. If I can't have you, then no one can," he whispers, his voice taking on a harsh, threatening edge.

"I got on the first plane out here only to find out that the address my PI dug up on Gabe was in a gated community. It's been a challenge getting to you, baby." He licks my cheek and I fight back the urge to gag, knowing that will only piss him off and make this so much worse. "But I'm nothing if not resourceful. Watching you the past few days, acting like this could really be your life, was fascinating, but I'm done waiting for you to realize how good you had it. You're an ungrateful bitch, ya know that? Now, should we wait until lover boy gets home so I can kill him in front of you, or should I just get started with you?"

A sob escapes at the same time I hear the sound of the back door sliding open, but I never hear it slide closed.

"Danae?" Wyatt's voice calls out.

"Fuck," Mitch whispers in my ear, gripping my jaw harder as if this is all my fault. "You stupid bitch. Just had to go and ruin all our fun, didn't you?"

He pulls my body back, pressing the knife tight enough to my skin that it pricks and a trickle of blood descends. He maneuvers us around the corner, out of sight of the kitchen just as I hear Wyatt enter. But he doesn't call for me, and even though I'm not a praying woman, all I can do is pray he notices the panic button on the counter and the tea bag that I'm pretty sure I dropped on the floor when I saw Mitch.

*Please let him realize Mitch has me.*

I whimper, and Mitch tightens up his grip again, the knife cutting me more and causing me to wince.

"Shut the fuck up," he whispers, his lips on my ear and his hot breath making me feel gross. "I'll kill you right now if you make another sound."

His voice is so low, it takes me a second to make out the words, but the threat in his tone is easy enough to understand.

Finally, I hear the sound of footsteps moving out of the kitchen and my heart plummets.

*No.*

*Okay, Danae. You're on your own. You got yourself into this, it's time to get yourself out.*

I think about all the ways that Gabe makes me feel strong, all the ways I always knew I could be, but didn't trust myself enough to truly *be* until he believed in me.

And I unleash.

I lift my leg and stomp hard on his foot at the same time that I wiggle my mouth and open my jaw wide enough to bite down as hard as I can.

"Fucking bitch," he curses, nowhere near as quiet as he's been, and I drop my weight until I land on my knees and elbow him in the crotch. He buckles and that's when I take my chance to run. I make it two steps before he lunges forward and grabs my ankle, causing my body to hit the ground hard. I kick furiously, unleashing all my built-up rage for the hell he's put me through over the past twenty-one months, finally giving him a good swift kick to his face which immediately has blood pouring out of his nose. His eyes turn murderous, but I don't wait to find out what he'll do to me next. I find my footing and run toward the living room. I can hear him hot on my heels, but I don't dare look back.

"I'm going to kill you, you fucking useless bitch."

# THIRTY-EIGHT

# Gabe

I speed the whole way home, unease swirling in my gut that something's not right. Call it intuition or gut instinct or whatever, but the second the game ended and I got back to the locker room and saw the text from Wyatt that they left early, I changed into my street clothes and got the hell out of there.

I'm about to turn into my driveway when my headlights flash on Danae running out the front door in her pajamas, blood trickling down her chest and her hair a mess. Fear fills her face and I understand why when two seconds later Mitch comes rushing after her. I only recognize his face from the photo of his driver's license that Wyatt got from Raff. Although the charismatic smirk in that photo doesn't match the deranged look on his face as he chases Danae out of my house with a knife in his hand.

I barely get the car in park before I throw the door open and rush out, screaming for Wyatt while I run toward Danae. At the sound of my voice, her gaze darts to me and she lets out a sob as she switches directions, running straight toward me. Fear lances my insides as Mitch rushes toward us, his knife raised and ready to strike. I do the only thing I can—I grab Danae and pull her against my chest, turning my back so that I'll take the brunt of Mitch's attack.

"Get down!" Wyatt's voice barely breaks through the adrenaline, but my reflexes are quick and I drop to the ground, taking Danae with me and cushioning her fall the best I can. At the same time, three gunshots ring out into the night, followed by a thud, and then silence.

The kind of silence that makes you wonder if you're still alive.

"Gabe, Danae, you guys alright?" Wyatt calls and I turn around to see him holstering his gun, his hand on Mitch's throat, but I don't know why he's even bothering. Mitch's eyes are lifeless as he lies on the ground with his blood already staining my grass.

Danae lifts her head to look and then curls into my arms, sobbing.

"It's okay," I say, my own heart still beating frantically from the close call. "I've got you. It's over."

"It's over," she sobs.

I nod, even though she can't see me, and I repeat, knowing we both need to hear it again, "It's over."

I only hold her like that for another minute before I pull us both up to a sitting position and my hands are everywhere, checking for injuries. Wyatt is already on his phone, likely calling either Raff or 911. Danae has two cuts that make my stomach turn—one near her collarbone and one a few inches down. I slide my fingers through her hair, holding her head in place as I stare into her honey-brown eyes.

"Mi reina," I choke out, dropping my forehead to hers and holding on to her. The police arrive, and then the paramedics. Wyatt talks to the police and then goes in the house with them while I get Danae looked over. Fortunately, none of the cuts are so deep that they need stitches. When Wyatt exits the house with one of the officers, I drop a kiss to Danae's head and say, "Be right back." I make a beeline for Wyatt, glaring at him, but reining myself in from throwing a punch at him for not doing his fucking job in the first place.

"What the fuck happened? *How* the fuck did this happen? You were supposed to keep her safe," I growl.

Wyatt runs his hand through his dark-brown hair. "I found one of the back doors unlocked when I did my sweep after we got back. I don't know how it got unlocked because I'd locked all the doors myself before we left. I had already cleared the rest of the house, and there'd been no sign of him. The police and I just found signs that he was possibly hiding in the crawl space entrance that you have in the closet of the downstairs guest bedroom. He would've had to get blueprints of your house to even know that was there."

"I have boxes in that closet from when I moved."

"I know. That's what tipped us off. They were all pushed out of the way, and he hadn't completely put the cover for the crawl space back on. He must've been hiding in there when I did my sweep. It's not standard that crawl space entrances are inside the house, so I'm going to see if I can find out how he knew about it."

"Where were you? How did he get to her?"

He runs his hand through his hair again and his face hardens in frustration—with himself or the situation, I'm not sure. "I was on the phone with Raff giving him an update and then I called Jaime to see if he had been to the house earlier at all to check things out while we were at the game and might've left the door unlocked. He hadn't and asked if anything else was amiss. It wasn't until I came back into the house and noticed the kitchen lights under the cupboards were on. When I called out for Danae, there was no response, but I thought I heard a noise, so I went to check, and that's when I saw her panic button on the counter and a tea bag on the floor. The water hadn't been turned on yet, but it was clear she was in the middle of something and should've been there."

He stops and looks at me, his gaze cautious. "How much of this do you really want to hear?"

"All of it." If she ever has nightmares about what happened tonight, I want to know every single detail so I can best support her through them.

"I heard a whimper on the other side of the wall."

My body itches to go back to Danae and hold her at the thought of her being held captive and being so scared she would whimper.

"Go on," I say, shaking away the horrifying image.

"I backtracked out of the room and was in the process of trying to sneak up on him from the other direction when I heard him curse and they got into some kind of scuffle." He chuckles. "She elbowed him in the dick, which would've hurt like a fucking bitch."

My gaze turns murderous. "You saw her struggling and you let her handle that herself?"

His face sobers. "I was looking for an opening to take him out, Gabe. If I'd jumped the gun he could've stabbed her. If I'd thought for one second that he was actually going to be successful in getting her back under his control after she got away, I would've taken the shot early. But it was dark and hard to see, and I wasn't going to risk shooting her on accident. When I saw her running out the door, I followed. Whether you had showed up or not, I wouldn't have let him touch her again. I promise you. But regardless, she's safe. It's over."

"She's traumatized!"

"No more traumatized than she already was by his taunting. He wanted to play with her, Gabe. He didn't want a quick kill. I took a calculated risk, and now that piece of shit is going in the ground where he deserves to be."

"I'm okay," Danae's soft voice says behind me, and I spin around just as she slides her arm around my waist. I pull her close to me, reassuring myself that she's all right.

The events of the evening come crashing down on me all at once—my fear for her safety, my disappointment in getting myself benched, then coming home to find her being chased by a madman—and tears fill my eyes as I drop my forehead to hers.

"I can't lose you, *eres mio, eres mi vida, eres todo, para siempre amor, para siempre*," I whisper, my throat thick. But every word is true. She is mine, my life, my everything, always.

"You won't lose me. He's gone now. It's over." She says the last part as if it's an answered prayer, which I suppose it is.

Letting out a relieved sigh, I kiss her forehead. "I love you."

"Te amo," she says, and hearing her speak Spanish for me nearly brings me to my knees with how much love I have for this woman.

"Should we expect the police to come back again in the morning?" I ask.

Wyatt shakes his head. "They'll get all their statements tonight." He glances back to the cops talking at the entrance to my house. "In fact, I imagine they'll be sending someone over here soon to get your formal statements. But it's pretty clear what happened. As far as they'll be concerned, it's a cut-and-dried case of self-defense. My recommendation is that you two go to bed once you've given your statements and try to get some sleep."

"I'm looking for a new house tomorrow," I announce, and Danae looks up at me, her eyes wide.

"What? Why?"

"I'm not living in a house where you'll be forced to live with the memory of what that monster put you through. It's just a house, mi reina. We'll find a new one—together."

"But that beautiful library you made for me—"

"I'll build you a bigger one. Hell, maybe I'll find you a real castle to live in and you can live out all your *Beauty and the Beast* dreams."

She smiles at me like I'm crazy, but doesn't argue with me, and I'm grateful she doesn't. Whether she thinks she can still live in this house or not, I can't. I'd always worry for her safety and think about this night if we were to stay here.

Brushing aside the house problem for tomorrow, we meet with the police and give our statements. Afterward, I carry her upstairs to our bed while Wyatt secures the house. Even with the threat gone, he's staying until we officially end the contract with Raff.

When we get up to our room, I go immediately to the shower and remove each article of her clothing with tender loving care. Under the hot spray of the water, her lips meet mine in a kiss that says a million things.

*I love you.*

*Thank you for being mine.*

*We're safe.*

*I need you.*

My hands caress down her body until I'm gripping her lush ass, and she lifts her leg to wrap around my hip. I take the hint and pick her up so she can wrap both legs around me, her slick heat rubbing teasingly over my already hard cock. I kiss down her neck until I get to the bandages.

"Shit. We should've covered these."

"It's okay," she says, brushing off my concern. "They aren't that bad. I can just put a new one on when we get out. Now shut up and kiss me."

I smile—my first since I got home, maybe my first all night—and do as she asks, kissing her until we're both panting.

"Oh," she says, pulling back. "Did you win? I can't believe I forgot to ask."

I smile wider now, finally allowing myself to feel joy tonight. "We did. We're heading to the Super Bowl."

She squeals and wraps her arms around me, but the motion also causes her body to rock deliciously on my dick, and I let out a groan.

"Fuck, keep doing that," I choke out.

"I want to do more," she whispers against my lips before kissing me deeply and moving one hand down between us to guide me inside her.

The second her warmth wraps snugly around me, I'm convinced I've found heaven on earth.

Words aren't strong enough to describe how she wrecks me and completes me all at once while she rides me like her release will cleanse us both of the trauma of tonight. I hold her ass in my hands and help her bounce on my cock until I feel the familiar rush that always hits me right before I'm about to come. The heaviness that comes over me until it narrows in on where my cock pumps into her perfect pussy.

I adjust her slightly so I can free up one hand and slide it between us, stimulating her clit. Her legs shake as she lets out a loud scream and tips over the edge, taking me with her as her walls squeeze around me, strangling my cock in the way only she can.

I collapse against the wall, my arms shaking as I hold her—more from the intensity of my release than actually holding her for an extended amount of time.

No one has ever been more perfect for me than Danae.

We finish our shower, washing each other reverently, and then lie down in bed, naked, sated, and snuggled together.

She melts against me, her head resting where my arm meets my shoulder and her hand on my chest. "You're my reward for all that I've gone through."

No, she's definitely the reward. One I plan to cherish for the rest of my life.

# Danae

EPILOGUE

Two Years Later

Gabe once asked me what I wanted to do with my life, and for the longest time I wasn't sure. I'd played around with some ideas after talking to Emma, but nothing really called to me. Then one afternoon as I sat in my new library in our new house—mansion, is more like it—words tumbled around in my head until the only way to make them stop was to get them down on paper. I spent three days writing damn near nonstop, and when I came out I had stinky breath, greasy hair, wrinkled clothes, and the first draft of what has now become a best-selling novel—my story of how I survived domestic abuse.

Women form a line in front of the table where I'm sitting, my hand is probably going to cramp any minute from how many books I've signed tonight, and yet I can't wipe the smile off my face to save my life.

Tears fill my eyes as another woman comes up to the table and hands me her book, telling me how my story gave her the strength to leave her verbally abusive ex. She's not the first one who's told me that tonight, and it never fails to make me feel both pride that I could be a part of their journey to a better life and fierce rage that there are so many men out there who seem to thrive on putting women down.

I vowed long ago that if I ever had a son, I would raise him to respect women, to understand the value of consent, to find his strength in raising people up instead of beating them down. As a society we have to do better for our sons and daughters. The success of my book has only reaffirmed that vow.

Gabe stands beside me, my constant protector, ready to come to my defense. On occasions when he can't be here, he'll hire Carmichael Security to place a temporary bodyguard for me. He knows there's no real threat any longer, but sometimes I think that night spooked him more than it spooked me.

For me, that was the night my nightmare died, but for Gabe it only made him realize how easily he could've lost me. I've brought him into my trauma therapy sessions several times so we could work on it, but it's a slow process.

I've quickly come to understand that Gabe's role in defending the backfield isn't only when he's playing football, but in his everyday life as well. He does all he can to protect and defend those he loves, none more than me, and it's a gift I will never take for granted.

The bookstore attendant shuffles over to me and leans down. "I'm so sorry this has gone past your time slot. I know you've been here several hours already. I can tell them you can't sign anymore and get you on your way."

I glance down the long line of women still left. "No, I'm okay." My hand's not cramping yet, and I know the importance of how much one person can change your life. If I'm that person for these ladies, I want them to know they're seen.

That they're not alone.

I greet each woman by their name once they tell me and sign their book.

*You're stronger than you think. Never give up.*

It takes another two hours before I sign the last book, and Gabe steps up to the table as the last woman turns around and walks away, holding the book tight to her chest like a lifeline and making me so glad I stayed, even if my hand's officially been cramping for the last half an hour.

"Tired?"

"Exhausted," I say, leaning back against the chair, all my muscles protesting after sitting for so long.

He holds out a hand—the titanium of his wedding band standing out against his tan skin—and I take it without hesitation. "Let's go home," he says, pulling me up from my seat and wrapping his strong arms around me. A deep sigh of satisfaction escapes as my hands slide up his broad chest. I've memorized all the tattoos under his shirt, kissed and licked every inch of his skin, and still it never feels like enough. I always want to explore him more, find something new about him, even if it's as small as a new wrinkle around his eyes from laughing so much.

He kisses the top of my head and then holds my hand in his as we exit the store. On the drive home, his hand rests on my upper thigh while my hand lies on top of his. My wedding ring glints every time we pass a streetlight, and a warmth blossoms from my stomach when I think about the absolutely perfect wedding day we had. We got married in a small intimate wedding on the beach in San Diego—the same beach where Gabe took me the night of his cousin's quince. We didn't have his or hers sides because it would've been grossly lopsided. Instead, we invited Gabe's family and the rest of the Fierce Four, as well as the women I'd grown close with over the season—Paige, Gina, Nikki, and Emma.

Our wedding was the first time he'd taken his Super Bowl Championship ring off since it was given to him when they won the Super Bowl that year. He insisted he didn't want any other jewelry to take away from his wedding ring because it was the most important piece of jewelry he'd ever wear.

As if I had any doubts. Some football players might prioritize football over family, but Gabe will never be one of those guys.

"How's your new book coming?" Gabe asks, interrupting my thoughts.

"Good. I'm almost done."

He glances at me before looking back at the road. "That was fast. You just started it two weeks ago."

"The words are flowing." That's an understatement. The story is screaming to get out so loudly I've been getting up after Gabe goes to sleep and typing for hours before my eyelids get so sandy and heavy, I can hardly keep them open.

"What's it about?" he asks as he pulls up to our house.

I loved Gabe's old house, but I love the house we picked out together even more. It's a perfect blend of our styles.

I roll my head on the head rest and look at him. "Want to read it?"

He smiles and looks at me with those deep-brown eyes of his. "How about you read it to me?"

Now it's my turn to smile. "You might blush."

That gets his attention. "What kind of book are you writing?"

"My favorite kind."

His smile slowly falls off his face as his expression morphs to hunger. "Reina," he chokes out. "Are you telling me you're writing a smutty book in that office of yours?"

I nod, which only causes him to growl, throw the car in park, and run around to my side. He pulls me out of the car and carries me bridal style into the house, all the while I'm laughing hysterically at his antics.

He heads straight to my office slash library and gently places me down on my feet before moving over to the couch. He sits down and spreads his arms across the back like he's a king in his castle.

"Maybe just skip to the dirty parts and then we can reenact them," he says with the sauciest little smile.

My heart swells until it feels like it's going to burst right out of my chest. I understand what the term "incandescently happy" means now, all because of Gabe.

My king.

Moving over and straddling him, I lean down and whisper in his ear. "Or I could just tell you the ending."

"Now where's the fun in that?"

Before I can come back with anything clever, he slides his fingers into my hair and pulls my mouth down to his, his tongue sweeping across my lips until they part with a gasp. He slides his tongue inside, salaciously licking into my mouth until I'm rocking against his thick erection and moaning shamelessly.

I push up his shirt with frantic motions, and as soon as he takes over pulling it off, I go for the button of his jeans. He shimmies out of his pants and underwear, leaving them piled around his ankles as I stand and pull my dress off in one smooth move. My bra and panties are gone in another blink and then I'm standing naked and exposed to him.

My husband.

My king.

My forever.

"Come here, mi reina. Let me worship you like you deserve."

And worship me he does. With his hands, his lips, his gloriously talented tongue. He lays me back on the couch and devours my pussy with such vigor that when he pulls my first orgasm from my body, I'm half convinced he just sucked my soul out of me.

When he finally slides inside, we both suck in a sharp breath. It never gets old, the feeling of him buried deep inside me, of loving me with every piece of him.

"Make love to me, my king," I plead, sliding my fingers into his soft, dark hair.

He shakes his head, his thick muscled arms holding him up from me, but our pelvises touching completely. "I'm not your king; I'm your servant." He kisses between my breasts. "I just want to worship every inch of you all the time."

I let out a soft exhale. "I love you, Gabe."

He kisses up my chest, my neck, my jaw, until he grazes my lips. "I love you, Danae, with everything I have."

We kiss deeply as he begins to rock inside me until we're both panting so hard that all we can do is moan into each other's mouths while we find bliss in each other's bodies.

"Fuck, I'm close."

He slips a hand between our bodies until he's sliding his thick thumb across my swollen clit. Three swipes is all it takes before my body detonates like an explosion and I shatter around him, pulling his orgasm out of his body as he releases inside me.

He collapses to the side, while his still semihard cock remains inside me and I nuzzle against his neck.

"Hey Gabe?"

"Hmm," he mumbles.

"Remember earlier before the signing when I told you I had a surprise for you?"

"Mm-hmm."

"Are you ready for it?"

He cracks open one eye. "That wasn't it?"

I shake my head and he opens both eyes. "It wasn't that you're writing steamy novels?"

"Nope."

"Then what is it?"

"I'm pregnant."

# Gabe

BONUS EPILOGUE

I couldn't have heard her right. Did she really say what I think she said? What I've been hoping and praying for since the moment I put that diamond ring on her finger?

"You're what?" I ask, worried I heard her wrong and just got all my hopes up.

She grabs my hand and brings it to her lips, kissing my fingers softly, her eyes sparkling with joy. "I'm pregnant, mi rey. We're going to have a baby."

I'm torn between melting into a puddle of emotion and soaring on cloud nine. Instead, I pull her against me in a fierce hug, holding this incredible woman—the love of my life and the mother of my child...*my child*. I don't know how the fuck I got so lucky to get her as my wife, but I silently vow to never take her for granted. To cherish every moment with her.

I drop a kiss to her head and then slowly pull out of her before carrying her up to our room. I don't care that we're both butt naked. All I care about is getting to our bed and making slow, passionate love to my wife. She owns every piece of me and I fully intend to show her just how much.

"I need to call a general contractor, or an interior designer. Yeah, an interior designer is probably a better fit for this job," I mumble to myself as I make my way to our room.

Danae's voice cuts through the planning already taking place in my mind. "Why do you need to call an interior designer?"

"To decorate the nursery. Maybe we should also get some help, like a housekeeper or two so you don't have to strain yourself doing anything."

Her eyes light up in that way where I know she finds me amusing and she pinches her lips together like she's fighting back a smile.

"Gabe, I'm pregnant, not debilitated. We're not hiring an interior designer for the nursery, although I probably won't turn down some extra help around the house once I hit third trimester, but ask me when we're closer."

"Are you sure?"

"I'm positive."

My shoulders sag a little with defeat as all the grand plans I'd already made in the last two minutes get thrown out the window. She must notice because she cups my face and asks, "What is it?"

I hold her a little tighter against me. "I just want to give you everything you want or need."

Because I'm holding her so close, I can feel the way her muscles relax at my words, and her gaze softens as she smiles up at me.

"Mi rey. You already do. You have from the very beginning. This life we have together is everything I've ever wanted, and *you* are all I need."

I drop my head to hers, kissing her softly as we finally get to our room before I place her on the bed and make love to her. I don't need any more words. All I need is her. Always.

Danae groans low—something her doula told her she should do instead of screaming because it would help the progress of the birth—and grips my hand so tight, she's liable to break it off if this continues much longer.

The contractions ramped up quickly, much faster than any of us thought they would for her first pregnancy. The nurses seemed to be moving in slow motion when I told them it was our first until they checked to see how dilated she was and how quickly things were progressing. Apparently, first babies take the longest to come out, but not our *princesa*. No, our little princess decided to make a grand—and swift—entrance.

It took less than two hours for Danae to start pushing, which honestly felt like an eternity for me, but the nurses told me it was much faster than usual. I don't care how long it takes; I just want my baby girl to be here already.

My wish is granted when Danae gives one more push and our daughter arrives. One nurse helps pull Danae's gown away from her chest as the doctor quickly lifts our now screaming baby girl onto Danae's chest for skin-on-skin contact. There's a flurry of activity as the nurses and doctor get Danae cleaned up and ready to deliver the placenta—something I didn't know about until our doula walked us through the process.

But none of the activity really registers because my gaze is locked on the sight of my gorgeous wife holding our tiny newborn daughter who has settled against her and seems perfectly content now that she can hear Danae's heartbeat.

Tears spill down my face as I rest my arm on the bed above Danae's head and drop a kiss to her forehead, my eyes still watching every tiny movement our daughter makes.

"Thank you, mi reina," I choke out, my emotions on full display. "She's perfect, just like you."

Peace has settled over Danae now that our daughter is here and she looks up at me with so much love, all I can do is kiss her to try and share an ounce of the love I feel for her in return.

It takes another hour or so before everything is done and the nurses are ready to help Danae get dressed so we can move to the recovery room where we'll be for the next day or two.

"Dad, you want to hold your daughter while we help mom?" The nurse asks me.

I stare at the tiny baby now wrapped in a blanket after being weighed and measured, then back up at the nurse.

"What if I drop her?" Panic seizes me. She's so small and delicate.

Both Danae and the nurse smile at me. "You won't drop her," my wife says, confidence radiating in her tone.

"Okay," I say, swallowing thickly and trying to suppress my nerves. The nurse picks up my tiny bundle of joy and places her in my arms.

"Just make sure you keep her head supported. There you go," she adds when I adjust my hold as necessary. This is nothing like practicing on the doll that our doula brought over.

"See, you're a natural."

My beautiful, tiny daughter—Alexa Sofia Romero— starts to whimper and panic grips me.

"Talk to her," Danae suggests as the nurse helps her sit up and get a new gown on her. "Let her hear your voice.

She'll recognize you from all those months you talked to my belly."

I look down at Alexa as her little nose scrunches up like she's getting ready to wail. "Now, now, my sweet princesa, don't cry." I begin to sing the familiar tune of a lullaby my mom sang to all of us when we were little.

*Duérmete mi niña*
*Duérmete mi amor*
*Duérmete pedazo*
*De mi corazón*

She quiets at the sound of my voice and then her tiny body stops squirming as she appears to fall asleep. My heart soars and I feel like the strongest man in the world that I can soothe this sweet little princess. I rock her in my arms, my gaze never straying from every minute detail of her face, how even now, I can recognize features that look like me and some that are so clearly from Danae. She's a perfect mix of the two of us.

"You ready, Dad?" The nurse asks as she reaches out to take Alexa and give her back to Danae, who's now sitting in a wheelchair with a serene smile on her face as she watches me with our daughter.

"Sure," I say, handing Alexa to the nurse.

Our walk to the room is fairly quick while Danae watches our daughter, held snuggly in her arms, and chats with the nurse. All the while, I'm reeling. It feels like my entire world has changed in a blink.

I'm a dad.

I'm a fucking dad.

And no title in the world will ever be more important than that one.

# AFTERWORD

I've had the idea for Gabe and Danae's book for years. I actually wrote the first chapter April 2021 because Danae's backstory, and that moment in chapter one in particular, came to me so strongly, I knew I had to get it down on paper.

It's always weird when I've finished a story for a set of characters who've lived rent free in my head for so long. It's bittersweet. I'm excited to finally get to share them with others, but also a little heartbroken that now their story is done. This one is no different.

I hope you enjoyed this story and if you've made it this far, thank you for your support. As an indie author, I couldn't do what I do without readers like you willing to take a chance on me.

I also owe a lot of thanks to the people who helped me behind the scenes.

To Kate, my amazing cover designer for this series. She never fails to deliver gorgeous covers for me.

To Ann Suhs and Ann Riza, my editors, for helping me make my stories really shine, for your timeline magic, and always catching when I overuse a word or phrase. I appreciate you both so much.

For my incredible friend and sensitivity reader, Rikki, thank you for giving me more insight into your culture and making sure I did Gabe and his family justice (and for helping me with all my Spanish phrases). I would be lost without you in general, but you definitely helped make this book what I hoped it would be.

To my husband, who never fails to tell everyone he meets (and I do mean, EVERYONE, including the nurses at his most recent doctor's appointment) that his wife is a romance writer and they should read my books. You are without a doubt the best hype guy and I love you so much. Thank you for making it easier for me to do this full-time.

To my children, my two little miracles who give me purpose and make my life better in every possible way, I love you so much. I hope you're never afraid to chase after your dreams.

I'm sure I'm forgetting someone, which I'm going to feel terrible about later.

These afterwords always make me a little emotional because I'm just so incredibly grateful to get to do this. To share my stories with you, to have the strength (and sometimes perseverance) to finish them, especially if the characters stop talking to me. So if you're still reading this (which blows my mind honestly), thank you for coming on this journey with me. I appreciate you so much.

# ABOUT THE AUTHOR

Cadence Keys writes steamy contemporary romance novels full of heart, heat, and HEAs. She loves football (especially seeing all those tight ends), coffee (it sustains her), and watching Gilmore Girl marathons (witty banter for the win). When she's not busy writing, she's spending time with her family or getting lost in a good book (always romance).

You can also find more information about all future releases at www.cadencekeysauthor.com/

facebook.com/cadencekeysauthor

x.com/cadencewrites

instagram.com/cadencekeysauthor

bookbub.com/profile/cadence-keys

goodreads.com/cadencekeysauthor

ALSO BY CADENCE KEYS

## LA WOLVES FOOTBALL

In the Grasp

Across the Middle

Down by Contact

Taking the Handoff

## LA WOLVES DEFENSE

Scorched Turf (author website exclusive novella)

Defending the Backfield

After the Snap

Closing the Distance

Protecting the Boundary

## RAPTUROUS INTENT ROCKSTARS

Noble Intent

Forbidden Intent

Devoted Intent

Promised Intent

## BREAKING THE RULES

Only a Kiss

Just for Tonight

About Last Night

## CFU HOCKEY

Campus Crush

Campus Rival

## MEADOWBROOK, MT

One Weekend in Montana

www.ingramcontent.com/pod-product-compliance
Lightning Source LLC
Chambersburg PA
CBHW061617190726
48288CB00007B/2356